THE SUICIDE SQUAD:
COFFINS FOR THE SUICIDE SQUAD
AND OTHER STORIES

ACE G·MAN

COFFINS FOR
THE SUICIDE SQUAD
AND OTHER STORIES

By Emile C. Tepperman

POPULAR PUBLICATIONS • 2022

THE SUICIDE SQUAD PAYS OFF

CHAPTER 1
BEGINNER'S LUCK IN HELL

BUSINESS WAS good tonight at the swanky Sunset Club, on the edge of Biscayne Bay. The winter season had started early. The hotels on Biscayne Boulevard in Miami proper, as well as those across the Causeway on Miami Beach, were well filled with pale anaemic men and women from the North who had come down in search of warm weather—and thrills.

But the race tracks hadn't opened yet, and only one dog track was operating. So in the evening the crowds sought their thrills at the dice and roulette tables of exotic places like the Sunset Club, where the smallest bet permitted was five dollars, and where Cuba Libras cost a dollar a piece.

The swing band was going hot and strong, and almost a hundred couples were dancing between courses. Later, when they finished dinner, they'd wander into one of the two gaming-rooms in the south wing of the Club. The dice table was already working in the Green Room, where half a dozen men in white evening clothes and as many women were eagerly testing their luck.

One of those patrons was a young fellow with curly hair and blue eyes. Unlike the other patrons, this young man had the intense and concentrated look of one who is intent on accomplishing some definite purpose. He was a little nervous, and his hand kept moving up toward a very noticeable bulge under his left armpit. He was trying to appear at ease, like the other players, but his very efforts to efface himself in the crowd around the table attracted attention to himself.

Two so-called "assistant managers"—who were really high-class bouncers in evening clothes—were watching him. So was the croupier at the dice table. Word had gone around the room that a cop was here.

The croupier raised his green eyeshade, and made a signal to the cashier, who sat in a cage in a corner. The cashier hurriedly came out with a drawer-full of money. One of the assistant managers walked with the cashier, and whispered to him, "Hurry up. That table's loaded with hot dough. Switch it quick!"

The cashier nodded and hurried across the room. But the dice had already come around to the curly-haired young man. He put a ten-dollar bill on the table, on the square marked, "To Win," and rolled the dice. The ivories bounced at the baseboard, and came to rest with a five and a two up. The croupier droned, "It's a seven. The gentleman *wins!*" He took a ten-dollar bill from the drawer and placed it on top of the young man's bill. He might have wanted to wait for the cashier to bring the other drawer of money, but it would have looked funny to the other patrons at the table. So he laid the money down.

The young man, instead of shooting again, picked up the two ten-dollar bills. He put his own away, and examined the one the croupier had given him. His face flushed as he studied the serial numbers.

The oilier patrons were not paying him any attention, for the one next to him had picked up the dice when he relinquished them.

He looked up and saw the cashier who had arrived at the table, and who was quickly exchanging the money drawers. A quick, hot light leaped into the young man's eyes. He hurried around the table to the croupier's box. But he never reached it. The two "assistant managers" had closed in on him swiftly, as soon as they saw him examining the serial number on the bill.

Suddenly, the young man stiffened as he felt the presence of the two thugs on either sick of him. Too late, he tried to go for his shoulder holster. They each had him by an arm. The thug on the right raised a hand and brought it down in a lightning motion. Something hard and vicious crunched against the young man's skull. He would have slumped to the floor if he had not been supported on both sides.

At the same instant, the cashier and the croupier, who were on the opposite side of the dice table, fell into a loud and vociferous argument about counting the money. The cashier insisted on counting the money in the drawer he was changing, and the croupier seemed to be insulted that his integrity was being questioned.

The patrons watched the argument with interest, not suspecting that it was being staged for their special benefit, to draw their attention from the two "assistant managers" who were dragging the unconscious young man, as if he were drunk, to a door at the

4

The sub-machine gun dropped

from the killer's hands!

rear of the gaming room. As soon as they disappeared through that door, the cashier and the croupier settled their argument amicably, and the play was resumed. No one noticed the absence of the curly-haired young man.

THE TWO bouncers half-carried, half-dragged the unconscious young man through the doorway and then along a narrow hall. One of them, who looked like a powerful bruiser, with a barrel chest and a bull neck, slung him over a shoulder, and carried him up a flight of stairs, with the other leading the way. They stopped before a door marked, *Manager's Office,* and the smaller one knocked.

"Who?" asked some one on the inside.

"It's me—Nick Fabian, Kris. Open up, quick. Bugs and me have caught a copper!"

There was a muttered curse within, and a moment later a lock clicked, and the door was opened by a tall, nattily dressed man, with a small waxed moustache, and black hair parted in the middle and pasted down with copious doses of hair tonic. His sharp, pin-point eyes flickered from Nick Fabian to Bugs, and the burden the latter was carrying. He quickly stood aside.

"Come in—quick!" he ordered.

He shut the door after them, and locked it, then motioned to a couch. "Put him there. What happened?"

Bugs dropped the unconscious young man unceremoniously on the couch, while Nick Fabian explained.

"He's a dick, Kris. He tumbled to the hot dough, and he started for the rest of it, so Bugs and me grabbed him and clipped him before he could start something. He was a push-over."

The young man was stirring. He moaned, and opened his eyes. For a second he was dazed, and then realization hit him. He sprang to his feet, clawing at his shoulder holster.

Bugs said, "Nuts!" and hit him again with the blackjack. This time the young man folded up for good.

"What the hell!" said Kris. "We got to cover up. We got to get rid of this punk."

"Do we knock him off?" asked Nick Fabian.

Kris didn't answer. For a moment he twirled the end of his waxed moustache. Then he knelt beside the unconscious dick, and started to go through his pockets. He took out the revolver and raised his eyebrows when he saw that it was a brand new .38 Service Special.

"He must be a beginner. His gun hasn't been used much."

Kris Mungo went through the other pockets, and found a wallet. He opened it, and whistled. There was a gold badge pinned inside it, and there was an identification card under the glassine window. The gold badge had lettering around the outside:

U.S. DEPT. OF JUSTICE
FEDERAL BUREAU OF INVESTIGATION

The identification card gave his name as Thomas Grant, Special Agent-in-training.

"Hell," said Mungo. "The guy's only a rookie. The Feds can't have anything on us if they only sent a rookie. He must have been making the rounds of the spots, just fishing for something. It's his hard luck he got a bite!"

"So well?" Nick Fabian asked impatiently. "Do we give it to him?"

"Not yet," said Mungo. "I better call the big boss."

He went to the phone, and lifted the receiver. When he got the operator he put his lips close to the mouthpiece, and whispered a number. He waited, drumming with his fingers on the desk-top. In a moment he had his party.

"Boss," he said, "this is Kris Mungo. We're in a jam here."

"What kind of jam?" asked a hard, authoritative voice.

"Well, I don't like to mention it over the phone. It's a Boy Scout."

"Boy Scout?"

"Yeah. You know—from Washington."

"Oh!" There was a second of silence. Then, "Did he get anything?"

"Yeah. But we got him here. We got to get rid of him."

"I see. All right. I'll be right over."

Mungo hung up, and nodded to Nick and Bugs. "The boss is coming over. Go downstairs and act as if nothing happened. I'll call you when I need you."

ACROSS THE Causeway, in a terrace apartment in Miami Beach overlooking the ocean, Mr. Humbert Considine hung up the phone with an impatient frown upon his cold, aristocratic face. He rang a bell, and a Jap butler appeared as if by magic.

"My hat, Yoshi," Mr. Considine said curtly. "And have the maroon car ready at once."

8

Downstairs in front of the building, two-hard-bitten men were standing at the entrance, and the maroon car was at the curb, with another grim-faced man at the wheel. As Mr. Considine came out, he said swiftly to the two men at the entrance, "Follow me. To the Sunset Club. Be sure no one is tailing us."

He got into the maroon car and said, "Sunset Club, Peavey," to the chauffeur.

When his car pulled away, the two men at the entrance went into the alley at the side of the house, and immediately pulled out, driving a grey sedan. They kept fifty feet behind Mr. Considine's limousine all the way across the Causeway, and up Biscayne Boulevard to the Sunset Club. They remained in the car when Mr. Considine got out and entered the club. Peavey, the chauffeur, went along with Considine, keeping just behind him, with a hand upon a gun in his pocket, and a sharp, wary look upon his face.

Mr. Considine nodded to the doorman, who saluted respectfully. Then he entered the lobby, but did not go into the main dining-room. He opened a small door at the left of the lobby, using a key of his own, and climbed a flight of stairs to Kris Mungo's office, with Peavey at his heel.

He rapped sharply at Mungo's door, and immediately it was opened. Mungo stood aside for him and Peavey to enter, then locked the door after them.

"There he is, boss," said Mungo, indicating the young G-man on the couch.

Young Thomas Grant was conscious once more. Mungo had

seated him upright on the couch, and had tied his hand's behind his back with picture-wire. He looked up with an attitude of grim defiance at Mr. Humbert Considine.

Considine listened a moment, while Mungo whispered the story in his ear. All the time that he listened, his cold eyes were fixed upon the young G-man. When Mungo finished he said, "Well, I guess it was the only thing to do. I'll handle it."

He came and stood close to the couch. "Well, Mr. Thomas Grant," he said, "it looks as if you uncovered something big. *Too* big."

Young Grant's lips were set tight. "That bill I got at the dice table was part of the ransom money from the Pincus kidnaping last August. You've been passing the ransom money out through your gambling houses, Considine. *You* were behind the Pincus kidnaping—and God knows how many others!"

Mr. Humbert Considine nodded gravely. "That's right, Grant. I admit it."

"You'll hang for it," said Grant.

Considine smiled. "I don't think so!"

Young Grant's face was pale. "I know what's in your mind, you devil. You're going to kill me. Well, that won't help you. The Field Office knows where I was working. We've had a dozen men out, looking for traces of that ransom money. When my body is found, they'll know who killed me."

"Maybe they will," said Considine. "But knowledge isn't enough. They have to *prove* it, in order to hang me. Don't forget, my young friend, that I am also a lawyer."

"That's what I can't understand," said Grant. "You're a clever lawyer. You could have made a good living at that. But it wasn't enough for you. You took over the rackets from the mobsters you defended. You control most of the slot-machines in Miami, and half a dozen night clubs like this one. But that wasn't enough, either, it seems. You also had to go in for kidnaping!"

Mr. Considine raised an eyebrow. "There are many things you don't understand, my young friend. And some"—he heaved a mock sigh—"that you never will. It's too bad you found that ten-dollar bill—too bad for you."

"You're crazy," blurted young Grant. "You can't kill me and get away with it. Everything will point to you. The Miami police are honest. They'll cooperate with the F.B.I. My murder will be laid on your doorstep—"

"Not the way I'm going to do it!" said Mr. Considine.

He turned away from the G-man, and nodded to Mungo, who picked up the phone and said into it, "Tell Nick Fabian and Bugs Nestor to come right up."

"Have Nick and Bugs take him down the back way," Considine ordered. "There will be a grey sedan in the alley, with two of my men in it. Put him in that car. Everything will be all right. Stop passing that hot money at the dice table for a couple of days."

He brushed an imaginary speck off the lapel of his white evening coat, smiled almost pleasantly at young Grant, and went out....

CHAPTER 2
THE SUICIDE SQUAD RESIGNS

FORTY-EIGHT HOURS later, five men were standing around a coffin in a mortuary parlor in the small town of Blakewell, North Carolina. One of the five was the local chief of police of Blakewell. The second was the Director of the Federal Bureau of Investigation of the United States Department of Justice. The other three were men whose names were poison to the underworld from coast to coast—Kerrigan and Murdoch and Klaw.

Those three were unofficially known as the Black Sheep of the F.B.I. They were never sent out on a routine assignment, but always rated the calls where death was practically a certainty. They were the Suicide Squad of the F.B.I. Not so long ago there had been five of them. Now there were only three. Tomorrow there might be only two—or one... or none. But one thing was sure—that when they died, they'd take their killers to Hell along with them.

Neither Kerrigan nor Murdoch nor Klaw said a word as they stood around that grim black coffin and looked down into the face of young Special Agent Thomas Grant. The mortician had done a pretty good job on him, but the scars of an ugly accident were still visible upon that young face.

It was the Director who spoke first. His voice was just a little shaky.

"Tommy Grant was the youngest member of the Bureau," he said. "He was found last night at the wheel of a wrecked car, on the road just outside of town. There was a half-filled bottle of whiskey on the seat alongside of him. Everything points to the fact that he was driving while intoxicated, and crashed."

Kerrigan and Murdoch and Klaw shifted uncomfortably, and glanced at each other. Then Stephen Klaw, the smallest of the three, cleared his throat. "I don't believe it, Chief. I knew Tommy while he was in training school. The kid didn't drink."

The Director nodded. "That's right, Steve. That's the reason I sent for you and Kerrigan and Murdoch. I have a job for you three—if you want to tackle it."

The three of them tensed, their eyes suddenly livening up.

"You think Tommy Grant was murdered?" big Johnny Kerrigan asked.

"Yes," said the Director. "I'm sure of it. He was working in Miami, not here in Carolina. He had a routine assignment out of the Miami Field Office, to check night clubs and gambling houses for ransom money from the Pincus and other kidnaping cases. He was covering Considine's clubs. The last night he was heard from, he was going to the Sunset Club. But everybody there swears he never showed up. We're supposed to believe that instead of working that night, he went out on a drunken spree, hired a car, and drove all the way up here—then crashed. The auto renting agency in Miami that owns the car, swears that the kid rented it. A gas station attendant in Georgia swears the kid stopped there and bought ten gallons of gas and a quart of oil."

The Director paused, and looked across the coffin of Tommy Grant at Kerrigan and Murdoch and Klaw. "Everything fits in beautifully—too beautifully. For my part, I'm sure Tommy was murdered—by Humbert Considine's men!"

"Then why not take them all in for questioning?" demanded Dan Murdoch, his dark eyes flashing. "A story like that could be broken by questioning all the employees separately—"

"You don't appreciate the cleverness of this crime, Dan!" the Director interrupted. "Tommy Grant's body was found here in North Carolina. All the evidence points to the fact that Tommy died right here. Therefore, the investigation falls under the jurisdiction of the North Carolina authorities. The F.B.I. has the right to investigate, also. But we have no right to go into Florida and make arrests unless we can find evidence to prove that Tommy died in Florida. The Miami police are eager to help, because they are also sure that Considine is responsible for Tommy's death. But if they tried to take in any of Considine's men for questioning, he could get a writ of *habeas corpus* at once. You see, Considine is too devilishly clever. By leaving Tommy's body in another state he has practically blocked any *legal* investigation in Miami."

Dan Murdoch suddenly smiled. "I see," he said softly. "I was wondering where we fitted in."

The Director's stern face softened momentarily. "I see I don't have to spell it out for you boys. The only way to break this case is by forcing Humbert Considine's hand in some way. It can't be done officially. *It can't be done by F.B.I. Agents.*"

Stephen Klaw's eyes were glittering. "In that case, sir," he said, "Special Agents Kerrigan and Murdoch and Klaw hereby tender their resignations from the Federal Bureau of Investigation—to take effect immediately!"

The Director smiled. "Your resignations are accepted," he said. "Under the law, you are permitted to recall your resignations within ten days, and rejoin the Service. I'll be waiting to hear from you. And I pray to God that you'll all three of you come out of this alive!"

As they stepped out of the mortuary chamber, he shook hands with each of them in turn. Then Kerrigan and Murdoch and Klaw walked solemnly down the street to Dan Murdoch's car, in which they had driven here from Washington.

From a pocket in the car, Dan Murdoch took a bottle of twenty-year-old Scotch whiskey, which he kept for such occasions. He filled three small paper cups.

They raised the cups to their lips. "To Tommy Grant," said Dan Murdoch. They drank.

Then Stephen Klaw took the bottle, and filled the cups again.

"And here," he said, "is luck to Humbert Considine—he's going to need it!"

IN ACCORDANCE with their usual custom, Kerrigan and Murdoch and Klaw never went into a town on a job together. Stephen Klaw arrived first by train. Kerrigan and Murdoch, who were driving in, would get here in two or three hours.

Klaw checked in at the Tamiami Hotel, only a block north of the Sunset Club, on Biscayne Boulevard. He stayed in his room only long enough to get two extra clips out of his bag for his two automatics, and went down into the lobby.

It was fairly busy down here. At one end of the lobby there

was a gay crowd of men and women, playing the slot-machines. Others were standing around and chatting, or sitting at small tables and drinking long cool drinks which were brought to them by waiters from the bar in the rear.

Stephen Klaw stopped by the desk for a moment, and surveyed the crowd. As he stood there, slim and wiry in white jacket and blue trousers, he might almost have been mistaken for a kid—were it not for those expressionless slate-grey eyes of his.

The clerk leaned over the desk and asked, "Is there anything I can do for you, sir?"

Klaw shook his head. Then he asked, "Whose slot-machines are those—Considine's?"

The clerk nodded. "Yes, sir. We used to have other machines, but after two stench-bombs were left in the cellar, we put in Considine's. They're not as good as the ones we used to have. Considine's machines are rigged so they only pay off about two percent."

"Thanks," said Steve. He left the desk and walked over toward the row of "one-armed bandits." There were eight of the machines, and they were all being busily played. There were two nickel machines, two for dimes, two for quarters and two for half-dollars.

An attendant with pockets full of coins stood at one side, making change for anyone who ran short of coins. This attendant was a heavy-set bruiser, and there was a noticeable bulge under his left armpit. His presence here was not so much for the convenience of the customers, as for the protection of the machines from damage by rival outfits.

Steve Klaw waited until one of the quarter machines was free. He went over to it and slipped a quarter in the slot. Then he pulled the handle sharply, but not all the way down, and pushed it back up again at once. The machine jammed. It was a trick he had learned in the F.B.I. research laboratory, where a complete study had been made of various gambling devices.

The player at the machine next to Steve's said, "Looks like it's busted."

Steve said, "Yeah." He began to pound at the face of the machine, and then began to shake it so that all the quarters in the jackpot box rattled.

The attendant pushed his way roughly through the crowd to Steve's side and growled.

"Hey, you! What you doin'?"

Stephen Klaw looked up at him. "It's jammed," he said mildly.

"Well, you don't have to bust it!" the attendant growled.

"Oh, no," said Steve. "I wouldn't want to bust it—much."

He shook it hard, and the machine started to topple off the stand. It swayed precariously, and the attendant yelled, *"Hey!"* and grabbed for it.

Steve gave it an extra shove, and it went over, hitting the floor with a resounding crash. It burst open, and a flood of quarters went cascading all over the lobby.

The customers jumped out of the way, laughing. Many of the women got down on their knees and began picking up the coins. They considered it a huge joke.

The burly attendant became red in the face. "You done that

on purpose!" he yelled, towering over Stephen Klaw. He put a big paw on Steve's shoulder. "I'll show you—"

"Take your hand off me," Steve said coldly.

"Wise guy, huh!" barked the husky. "Well, see how you like this!" He kept his left hand on Steve's shoulder, and swung a wicked right at the G-man's jaw.

Klaw twisted away from the blow with effortless ease, and dug a left hook into the bruiser's stomach. Almost at the same time, like a snake flicking up at a victim, his right crashed into the other's jaw. That blow was deceptive. To anyone who saw it, it did not seem possible that Stephen Klaw's slim body could pack so much dynamite. The bruiser's head snapped back, and he went tottering backward, among the quarters and the debris of the wrecked machine, clawing for balance.

Steve grinned wickedly, and followed him up with a right deep into his stomach that sent him hurtling back into the row of machines. The big man hit them hard, and three of the one-armed bandits went crashing to the floor on top of him.

Stephen Klaw massaged his knuckles. "So sorry," he said to the hotel manager, who had come running out hastily. "Some one ought to teach better manners to these slot-machine gangsters."

The manager was groaning. The clerk had whispered to him that Klaw was a guest. "This is terrible, sir. You've made a lot of trouble for yourself. You don't know how vicious these thugs are. I wish I didn't have to keep the machines here. They'll surely do you harm, sir. Considine will be in a murderous rage when he hears that four of his machines have been wrecked. Perhaps you had better move—"

"On the contrary," Steve said smoothly. "I insist that when Considine inquires, you tell him that the damage was caused by—Stephen Klaw!"

He left the manager open-mouthed, and strolled out of the hotel.

CHAPTER 3
A LITTLE GAME OF STUD

S TEPHEN KLAW walked down Biscayne Boulevard, but avoided going into the Sunset Club. He turned west on Flagler Street, however, and entered a narrow building over whose door there was a sign reading, "Nick's Coffee House."

There was a narrow flight of stairs to the upper floor. Here, a thin-lipped gunman stood on guard before a door.

"Where to, mister?" he asked.

"I crave," Steve said, "to play some stud poker."

The guard studied him, narrow-eyed. "I ain't seen you here before."

"I just came down from the North," Steve said. "A friend told me to look this place up. He said to ask for Sammy Lax."

"Okay" said the guard. "You can go in."

Steve opened the door and stepped inside. He found himself in a huge room, thick with cigarette smoke. There were almost a hundred men present.

At one end of the room, across the entire wall, there was a

huge blackboard, upon which were marked the names of every race track in the country operating at the time, with the names of the horses and jockeys.

During the daytime, this place was a book-making office. In the evening, it was a gambling-room. At the rear there was a row of windows, closed now, where patrons made their bets and were paid off. In the center of the room there were three busy dice tables, with sweating men crowded around them. No women were permitted here. At the left, there were three smaller tables, at which intent men were playing stud or faro. Each table had a house man dealing, and the house took a cut from each pot. Circulating around the room were five or six tough-looking thugs, with guns bulging under their coats. They were here to keep order, and to protect the large amounts of cash at the dice and card tables.

A big, fat man with a double chin came over to Steve. "Welcome, stranger," he said. "I'm Sammy Lax. Just call me Sammy. Looking for a game?"

"A little stud," said Steve.

"Sure. We got two stud tables. One's a dollar and two. The other's five dollars in the kitty each deal, and table stakes."

"I'll take the table stakes," Steve told him.

"You got to buy a hundred-dollar stack."

"Suits me." Steve took out a thick roll of bills.

Sammy Lax's eyes brightened. "Come right along, stranger." He put a fat arm around Steve's shoulder, and led him through the fog of smoke to the stud table. As they walked, he pressed a little close to Steve, and his hand brushed, as if by accident, against Steve's hip pockets.

At the table he said to the five men already playing, "Here's a sixth, boys." He patted Steve on the shoulder, and his hand touched lightly but surely at the spot where one would carry a shoulder holster. Apparently satisfied that the newcomer had no weapons, he pulled out a chair for Steve, who seated himself, and handed a hundred dollars to the house man, who gave him a stack of chips.

The players were all silent and intent upon their game. They nodded to Steve, sizing him up covertly. At least three of them were professional gamblers employed by the house, sitting in the game on the chance that a sucker would come in. Then they would raise the pot when one of them had a good hand, thus drawing attention away from whichever one of them had the winning cards. Steve could tell that they were busy estimating how much money he had with him.

He went into the first few hands on everything, dropping forty dollars in ten minutes. He lost one large pot on three aces, to a low straight, and the dealer said, "Tough luck, bud. I was sure you were tops."

Steve shrugged. Negligently he asked, "This isn't one of Humbert Considine's spots, is it?"

He could see the other men at the table stiffen. The dealer's swift and agile hands faltered for an instant in dealing, then proceeded smoothly.

"Why do you ask?" the dealer demanded sharply.

"Just out of curiosity," Steve said. "I've heard that Considine is a dirty crook. I wouldn't want to play in one of his houses. They say all his dealers are crooked."

THE DEALER didn't answer. He kept on passing the cards around, and Steve got a king in the hole, and a deuce showing. His next card was a deuce, giving him a pair. He bet five dollars. All the others stayed. Steve's next card was a king, and another player, whom the rest called Al, got two sevens and a queen showing. Al bet five dollars, and Steve raised it twenty. Al saw the bet, and one of the other players unexpectedly raised the pot fifty dollars. Steve had just fifty dollars worth of chips in front of him. He pushed them in.

"You can buy more chips if you need them," the dealer said. "Or you can have me deal the hand out at table stakes."

"I'll buy more chips after the next card," Steve said.

The dealer nodded, and dealt. Al got another seven with his queen and two sevens, giving him three of a kind showing. Steve got another king, giving him three kings full.

Al, who had the highest hand showing, bet twenty dollars.

"Your bet, mister. Want to buy more?" The dealer asked Steve.

STEVE PUSHED his chair back a little. His hands were dug deep in his jacket pockets. His slate-grey eyes were absolutely without expression. But there was a hard smile at his lips.

"No," he said, speaking very loud, so that his voice carried above the hubbub at the dice tables. "I'm not buying any more chips. This is a clip joint. You dealt that last round of cards off the bottom of the deck!"

There was a sudden deadly hush in the huge room. Even the rattle of the dice ceased.

In that hush, Steve leaned across the table, taking his left hand out of his pocket, and flipped over Al's hole card. It was a seven.

Steve put his hand back in his pocket. "Four of a kind!" he said. "Against a full house. What a spot for a killing!"

The dealer snarled, "Why, you little punk! You say I dealt crooked? I'll push your teeth in—"

He stopped, looking at the big, flabby figure of Sammy Lax, who had come up to the table. Behind Sammy Lax, the four or five gunmen-guards were converging on the table.

Steve Klaw stood up, keeping his hands in his pockets.

Sammy Lax looked at him with a hurt expression. "Now, mister, I'm sure you know better than to come here looking for trouble. If that's what you're after, we can give it to you."

"Trouble," said Stephen Klaw, "is exactly what I'm after."

He kicked the chair out of the way, and took two quick steps to the left, setting his back against the wall. His two hands came out of his pockets, each gripping a small black automatic. One of the guns centered on Sammy Lax's stomach. The other moved in a narrow arc, covering the converging gunmen, who had also drawn guns.

Klaw's glance swept the room.

"Well," he asked. "Who wants to start giving me this trouble? Or do I get my money back?"

One of the gunmen at the extreme left raised his revolver in a lightning motion, thinking that Steve wasn't looking at him. But Klaw flipped his wrist around, and pulled the trigger.

His automatic barked before the gunman could fire, and

the man cried out hoarsely and dropped the revolver. His face became green with pain, and he hugged a shattered right arm against his side.

That was the signal for pandemonium to break loose in the place. The players around the dice tables began to mill all over the room, some making for the door, others crowding against the croupiers. Eager hands dug into the money boxes of the croupiers at the dice tables, plucking out handfulls of bills. This was a chance that came only once in a lifetime—a fight in a gambling-house, with the guards busy, and no one to stop them from helping themselves!

Steve Klaw had not remained stationary after firing that one shot. He jumped forward and got a grip of Sammy Lax's coat. He yanked the big man off balance, swung him around and pulled him in front of himself as a shield against the guns in the room. He kept one of his automatics against Sammy's spine, and thrust the other one menacingly out in front of the big manager.

"All right, Sammy," he said. "Tell your stooges to scram."

Sammy Lax was groaning. "My God, they're taking all the dough! There's fifty grand in this room, an' they're taking it all away!"

THE GUNMEN had been closing in, trying to get a shot at Klaw past the manager's bulk. Now, at Sammy's shouts, they turned belatedly to protect the money boxes. But they were all empty, and the crowd was streaming out like a flood.

Stephen Klaw took swift advantage of that momentary shift in the attention of the gunmen. He gave Sammy Lax a hard shove, and sent him sprawling to the floor. Then he swung around and kicked over the stud table at which he had been playing, and which was deserted now. Then he raced across the room toward the milling stream of men who were pushing out through the doorway.

One of the gunmen saw him and yelled, "There goes that punk!"

He fired as he yelled, and the slug whined past Steve's head, smashed into one of the men massed in the doorway. Steve snapped a shot which caught the gunman in the shoulder, whirling him around like a top. Now the others were turning their fire on Steve, disregarding the fact that every bullet that missed him buried itself in one of the men in the crowd.

Steve's eyes became grim. Instead of trying to get out, he sprang back across the room, and up-ended one of the long dice tables. He leaped behind this, with a fusillade of shots following him, and used it as a barricade. He crouched behind it, with only his head showing, and fired methodically and coolly, shooting not to kill, but to disable.

His two guns kept blazing twin streams of lead at the gunmen. There were only two of them left on their feet now, and these two decided it wasn't worth it. They turned and ran toward the rear, disappearing through a door alongside the pay-off windows.

The room was cleared now, except for the wounded gunmen, and one of the patrons, who was hit in the leg. The rest of the customers had gotten away with all the cash in the place.

Sammy Lax was picking himself up from the floor, and clawing at a gun in his hip pocket. Steve Klaw grinned thinly, and came over to him.

Sammy saw him coming, cursed, and got the gun all the way out.

Steve covered the last three feet in a running leap, and smacked down with an automatic upon Sammy's wrist. Sammy Lax howled, and dropped the gun. Steve pocketed his automatics, as he heard the sound of a police siren out in the street. He grinned at Sammy Lax.

"When you see Humbert Considine," he said, "tell him the guy who wrecked his place is Stephen Klaw!" He stepped in close and brought up a sweet uppercut to the big man's chin that laid him down on the floor.

Then Steve turned and sprinted for that back door through which the gunmen had fled. It led out into a backyard, and by the time the police got upstairs, Stephen Klaw was out on First Street, which runs parallel to Flagler. He was whistling very contentedly as he stepped into a dark doorway and inserted new clips in his automatics....

CHAPTER 4
A HOOD FROM DETROIT

IT WAS now nine P.M., and the crowds were out thickly on Biscayne Boulevard. The restaurants and cafeterias were busy, and busses were picking up hundreds of people headed for the Dog Track. Steve had two hours more in which to work, because Kerrigan and Murdoch couldn't possibly get in before eleven.

He got a cab, and drove over the County Causeway, which links Miami to Miami Beach, across Biscayne Bay. Considine had a number of spots on the beach, and Steve visited two or three of them, causing considerable damage and confusion at all of them, and being careful to leave his name at each.

Then, about a quarter of eleven, he headed back to his hotel.

The clerk looked at him queerly when he got his key. Steve grinned, glancing at the row of newly installed machines in the lobby. There was a new attendant in charge of them, who carefully avoided looking at Steve. Also, there were three or four hard-faced men lounging in the lobby, with an elaborate appearance of idleness.

Steve grinned at the clerk. "I see Considine works fast," he remarked. "He must have a lot of machines in reserve."

The clerk was worried. He glanced furtively around to see if he was observed, then he said swiftly. "I wouldn't go upstairs if I were you, Mr. Klaw."

Steve raised his eyebrows. "Thanks for the tip." He took out a ten-dollar bill and slipped it across the counter. "Buy yourself a slot-machine with that. And if two men by the name of Kerrigan and Murdoch come asking for me, give them a duplicate key to my room, and send them up without delay. Okay?"

"Thank you, Mr. Klaw," said the clerk.

As Steve made for the elevator the clerk looked after him as one looks after a dear departed friend.

At the fifth floor Steve got out of the elevator and went to the door of 517, his room. He glanced up and down the corridor, making sure there was no one lying in wait out here. He noisily inserted the key, and turned it. He turned the knob, pushing the door open just a crack. Then he stuck both his hands in his jacket pockets, and kicked the door wide open.

Two men were visible to him inside the room. The one sitting on the bed had dun-colored hair, and a split lip. The one sitting on the chair by the window had a toothpick in his mouth. Both of them had guns, and the guns were trained on the door through which Stephen Klaw came.

"Keep comin' in, mister," said the one on the bed. "Don't stop."

Steve stopped, standing alongside the half-open door. He looked nonchalant, with his hands in his pockets.

"What do you want?" he asked them.

The one with the toothpick grinned. "You're the guy that's been goin' around town raisin' hell and giving the name of Stephen Klaw?"

"That's right."

"Well, the boss wants to talk to you. You're coming with us."

"Who's your boss—Considine?"

Split-lip growled, and got up from the bed. He kept the gun pointing at Steve. "You'll find out—plenty. Turn around while I frisk you."

"Perhaps," said Steve, "it would be better for you both if you put away your guns and went out of here now."

Split-lip growled again. "Come here, Looney," he said to the one with-the toothpick, "and keep him covered while I frisk him."

"Okey-doke, Mike," said Looney. He got up from the chair and came over to the door, with his gun handy. "Stick up your mitts, punk. The boss said to bring you back in one piece—if possible. If not, to leave you stiff. So take your choice."

"I'm sorry," said Stephen Klaw. "Very sorry to have to do this."

He shot from his pockets—once with each gun.

Looney took the slug high in the shoulder, where Steve had intended it to go. But unfortunately, Mike moved sharply to one side at the moment when Steve fired, and the bullet caught him square in the heart instead of in the shoulder.

He dropped like a ton of bricks, while Looney gasped with the shock of the impact, and slumped against the wall. He let the gun fall from his nerveless fingers, and just stared at Steve with a stunned look.

STEPHEN KLAW came all the way into the room, and kicked the door shut. He pocketed his automatics, and pushed Mike's body out of the way. Then he helped Looney over to the bed. He laid him on it, and helped him off with his coat, then ripped away the shirt.

The wound was bleeding freely. The bullet had gone through the fleshy part of the shoulder, and come out at the back.

"I guess you'll be all right," Steve told him. "Lie still till I fix you up."

He opened one of his bags and took out bandage and iodine. He got hot water and a towel from the bathroom, and washed the wound, cleansed it, and bound it up.

Looney lay quietly with his eyes closed while Steve worked over him.

"Thanks, pal," he said. "It's more than I'd do for you."

"Don't mention it," said Steve. "You're going to do a lot for me before I'm through with you."

"What do you mean?"

"You're going to help me get Considine."

"Nuts," said Looney. "I ain't no rat."

"You will be," Steve assured him.

He took a pair of handcuffs from his bag, and cuffed Looney's left wrist to the bed post.

Looney's eyes widened at sight of the bracelets.

"Hey! Are you a cop? We thought you was a trigger guy trying to muscle in on the boss's territory."

"I'm not a cop," Steve told him truthfully.

"Then—then how did you get these bracelets? They're official handcuffs."

Steve grinned. "They used to belong to a G-man."

Looney exclaimed. "You're a hard guy, ain't you?"

"What do you think?"

Klaw didn't give him a chance to answer that one. He had changed to another coat while he was talking, and had taken two more extra clips from the bag. He started for the door.

"Listen," Looney called after him. "You gonna leave me here for long?"

"Not long," Steve told him, and went out and locked the door after him.

He took the elevator down to the lobby, and saw Kerrigan and Murdoch at the desk, inquiring for him. Also, he saw the astonished looks on the faces of the four or five men who had watched him go up, and who were obviously planted there by Considine.

Johnny Kerrigan saw him, and started to call out across the lobby, but Steve just raised one eyebrow, and kept on walking. Johnny took the hint, and turned back to the desk, nudging Dan Murdoch. The clerk started to point Steve out to them, but Johnny Kerrigan said something to him quickly, and he stopped.

Stephen Klaw crossed the lobby, passed the slot-machines, which were still getting a heavy play, and went into one of the telephone booths. From inside the booth he could command a view of most of the lobby, and he saw two of Considine's men inconspicuously following him. One of them sidled into the adjoining phone booth.

For this one's benefit, Steve picked up the receiver, but held the hook down. In a loud voice he said, "I want to get Detroit!"

Then he released the hook and gave the operator the number of the Tamiami Hotel. In a moment he saw the clerk at the desk pick up the phone, and heard the clerk's voice say, "Tamiami Hotel, good evening."

"Let me talk to Mr. Murdoch—one of the two men at the desk," Steve said.

He saw the clerk hand the phone to Dan Murdoch.

"Dan!" he said swiftly. "Hold on a second."

He covered the mouthpiece, and raised his voice for the benefit of the man in the next booth. "Detroit? I want a person-to-person call to Jack Slade, in the Imperial Hotel!"

Jack Slade was the number one racket boss of Detroit, and

Steve knew this would impress the eavesdropper. Then he removed his hand from the mouthpiece, and lowered his voice.

"Dan, there are two lobsters up in my room. One is broiled, the other is kicking. Get the key and go up and talk to the live one. I'm going to the Sunset Club. Tell Johnny to tail me, and watch for the cue to start action—"

"Nix, Shrimp," said Dan. "We'll both tail you. Let the lobster wait upstairs. How you been doing?"

"Pretty good. I've got Considine after me. There are four or five gorillas right here in the lobby. They're kind of wondering what happened to their two pals upstairs. I think I see one just going up to investigate. Listen, Dan, you go up and handle him, and let Johnny cover me. You can come over later. I'll wait fifteen minutes before starting fireworks."

"Okay," said Dan. "But if you start without me, I'll wring your neck, Shrimp."

"Okay, Mope," said Steve. "Hang up."

Dan Murdoch hung up, as Steve clicked the hook down, and raised his voice once more. "Hello," he fairly shouted. "Is this Jack Slade? How are you, Jack? This is Steve. Say, I'm going to town on Considine's layouts. We'll have him eating out of our hand in no time. Yeah, everything is jake. Better send a bunch of the boys over by plane."

He kept on his imaginary conversation for another minute or so, and then hung up.

HE STEPPED out of the booth, and the eavesdropper came out of the adjoining one and fell in step beside him, and the other Considine man, who had been standing near by, fell in step at his other side.

"Just keep walking, bo," said the one at the left. He was getting the gun in his coat pocket into position against Steve's ribs as he spoke, and he was unprepared for Steve's quick reaction.

Steve simply stopped walking, and the two hoods couldn't help but finish the step they had begun to take. That put them slightly ahead of Steve.

Steve's two automatics came out of his pockets. He held them low, where they couldn't be seen by the patrons in the lobby, and pointed them at the two thugs. They turned their heads, and froze where they stood.

Steve grinned at them disarmingly. "Take your hands out of your pockets—empty!" he ordered.

Slowly, the two men brought their hands out, and held them in plain view.

"Nice boys," said Steve. "Now, keep walking. Scram out of here. Next time I see either of you, I'll shoot on sight."

"Listen," said the one who had eavesdropped. "You're nuts if you think you can muscle in. Now we know who you are. You're one of Jack Slade's Detroit mob. Well, you guys can't come in here and take over. Our boss is too big for you. If you guys want in on the racket, why don't you come over and talk it over with the boss? He might give you a piece of territory. There's plenty for everybody down here."

"Nix," said Steve. "We like the slot-machine racket, and the gambling spots. But we ain't tying up with any outfit that goes in for snatching. That's a Federal rap."

He slipped the automatics back in his pockets, but kept his hands on them. Out of the corner of his eyes he saw that Dan Murdoch had taken the elevator up, and that Johnny Kerrigan was watching him out of the corner of his eye.

The Considine hood at his left tried again. "Hell, how do you know about snatching?"

Steve grinned. "We get around a lot. And we hear a lot. The Feds are going to come down on your boss like a ton of bricks. We hear Considine has been passing the hot snatch money through his gambling spots, and a G-man tumbled, and he knocked off the G-man. Well, when your boss gets the works from the Feds, we're gonna be right here on the spot to take over the rackets!"

The hood looked terribly worried.

"That Pincus snatch was a bad one," Steve said. "And killing the G-man was a dumb move."

"Hell," said the hood, "nobody can put the finger on us for that. The boss is too smart. He's a lawyer."

"Well," said Steve, "let's go up to my room first."

The hoods looked at each other, and shrugged.

"Okay, pal. Maybe we can convince you. You got the drop on us, anyway."

The three of them started for the elevators, with Steve just a little behind.

The other Considine men in the lobby had been watching closely, and they had caught the by-play with the guns. They were converging slowly toward Steve and his two new acquaintances, and Johnny Kerrigan was moving around so as to get a point of vantage.

But the hood at Steve's left, who was apparently in command, shook his head almost imperceptibly in the negative, and the other gunmen let them go. They got into the elevator and rode up to the fifth with Steve still keeping behind them.

"You don't have to worry," said the spokesman of the two when they got out of the elevator. "As long as we're gonna talk this over friendly like, you don't have to worry that we'll jump you."

"I'm not worried," Steve told them. He took out his two automatics "I'm just playing safe." He prodded them along to the door of 517, and kicked it.

"Who?" asked Dan Murdoch.

Dan opened the door. He grinned when he saw Steve's two companions.

"A regular round-up, eh, Shrimp?"

"In!" Steve ordered the two hoods, motioning with his automatics.

THE TWO gunman began to suspect they had not been invited up here just for a conference. When they got inside and Dan had closed the door they became certain of it. They stared from the dead body of Mike to the manacled figure of Looney on the bed.

Stephen Klaw kept them covered while Murdoch frisked them both.

"This one," said Steve, indicating the hood who had done all the talking, "knows about Considine's snatch racket. He also

35

knows something about the bumping of that G-man. I think you'll have to stay here, Dan, and sort of keep an eye on them, while Johnny and I go over to the Sunset Club." He grinned. "Too bad, Dan. Looks like you'll miss the fun."

Murdoch had a sour look on his face. "Damn you, Shrimp, the next time we go on a job, *I'm* getting the action!"

"In the meantime," Steve continued imperturbably, "you can talk to these—gentlemen, and see what you can learn."

He took the elevator down, and came out into the lobby. He almost burst out laughing at the expression of blank amazement on the faces of the remaining Considine men down there. They had certainly not expected Klaw to come down alone this time.

Steve walked past them as if he didn't know them, winked at Johnny Kerrigan who was standing near the door.

He walked down one block toward the Sunset Club. Once he glanced behind him, and saw the Considine men following him in a tight group about fifty feet behind, and Johnny Kerrigan ambling along behind them. Everything was going fine so far.

CHAPTER 5
GUNS AT THE SUNSET CLUB

K LAW WAS one of a dozen people entering the Sunset Club, some from taxicabs, others from nearby hotels. It was almost midnight, and the last race at the dog track was over, so the crowds were streaming back into Miami.

Steve came into the foyer of the club behind a party of two men and three women, and the doorman didn't even notice him.

He followed the crowd across the dining-room toward the south wing, where the gambling-tables were located.

Steve wandered around for a few minutes, watching the entrance. Right after he came in, he saw the group of Considine thugs enter. They spotted him at once, and spread out around the room so as to be on all sides of him.

Steve acted as if he had not seen them. But he made sure to keep one hand in a pocket at all times. Two minutes more, and he saw Johnny Kerrigan's big stevedore shoulders appear in the doorway.

Steve started to push his way in toward one of the dice tables.

The two "assistant managers" suddenly appeared at the fringe of the crowd, and one of them tapped him on the shoulder. Steve did not know him at the time, but it was Nick Fabian. The other one was Bugs Nestor.

Steve frowned, and turned around, looking up at Fabian's brutal face.

"Well?" he asked.

"Excuse me, mister," said Fabian. "Have you got a card of admission?"

Steve raised his eyebrows. "Who ever heard of a card of admission to a dump like this?"

He said it in a very loud voice, so that all the people pressing around the dice table heard him. Several of them turned to watch, scenting a fight, perhaps thinking it was a noisy drunk who was going to get the bounce.

Nick Fabian's face broadened in an ugly scowl. "Look, mister, I think you better get out of here. You ain't wanted here."

He put a hand on Steve's shoulder to turn him around.

Stephen Klaw turned all right—but much faster than Fabian had expected. His left fist came around with all the force of his lithe body behind it, and slammed into the side of Fabian's face. The knuckles cut a raw line in his cheek.

"I don't like anyone to put his hands on me!" Steve said.

Fabian's eyes were murderous. He wiped the blood from his cheek, and came in at Steve. Suddenly, a circle was cleared around them. The only other one near them was Bugs Nestor, who was a little behind Steve. Fabian signaled to Nestor with his hand, and Nestor yanked his gun out and stepped in toward Klaw.

But someone else stepped in much faster. Big Johnny Kerrigan came up behind Nestor on noiseless, gum-soled shoes, and got a grip on his gun arm with the powerful fingers of his right hand. He whispered in Nestor's ear.

"Let it be a fair fight, pal."

Nestor squirmed in that crushing grip, but he couldn't get enough strength back in his arm to raise the gun.

In the meantime, Nick Fabian had his own gun out. He began, "Now you punk, we'll see—"

He didn't get any farther, because Stephen Klaw suddenly had an automatic in his hand, and the automatic was smashing down at Fabian's wrist. It struck bone with a crunching sound, and Fabian's snarling challenge changed to a cry of pain.

Steve said, "So sorry, mister. I forgot to tell you I also don't like people shooting me!"

He took Fabian's gun out of his resistless hand, broke it, and took the cartridges out. He put them in his pocket, and threw the revolver carelessly on the floor. Then he turned and faced the room.

"Any one else want to try something?" he asked.

"Look out, Shrimp—to your left!" yelled Johnny Kerrigan, and at the same time he sent Bugs Nestor hurtling away from him with a powerful shove, and threw down his gun on a small group of croupiers and guards who had pulled guns and were coming in at Steve from the left.

Johnny fired five times quick, and Steve, moving more by reflex motion, swiveled and fired in the same direction, his shots blending their raucous thunder with those of Kerrigan's.

The gunmen scattered under that blast, leaving two of their number writhing on the floor.

Men and women patrons began to mill around in panic. Women screamed above the thunder of the guns, and men tried to shield them with their bodies.

"This way, Shrimp!" shouted Johnny Kerrigan, backing toward the door at the side, which led to the upper floor. He kept his gun belching at the gunmen, and Steve brought out his second automatic and joined the chorus, backing toward Kerrigan.

Kerrigan reached behind him and yanked the door open, and they both slipped through.

Steve turned and grinned at Johnny. "Nice going, Mope."

"Not bad, Shrimp, not bad," said Johnny Kerrigan. "How about we go upstairs and see what makes this club tick?"

"Good idea," said Steve.

THEY STARTED up the flight, and a door at the head of

the stairs opened. Kris Mungo appeared. He had a burnished sub-machine gun in his hands, and as soon as he saw Klaw and Kerrigan he dropped flat on the floor of the landing up above, and poked the muzzle of the gun over the edge.

"Drop your rods," he ordered, "or I'll spray the two of you!"

Steve and Johnny squinted up toward the landing, but there was nothing to be seen of Mungo to shoot at—only the muzzle of the Thompson.

Steve said hurriedly to Johnny, "He'll have to lift his head up to shoot. I'm going up after him. When he raises his head, you pot him!"

He didn't give Kerrigan a chance to argue, but launched himself up the stairs.

"You damned fool, Shrimp!" Kerrigan shouted. His own gun was empty, and he knew that both of Klaw's clips were exhausted. They didn't have a chance.

Steve covered three or four steps of the flight, and Mungo, who dared not show his head to aim after what he had heard, blindly pulled the trip of the sub-machine gun. The muzzle was elevated far too much, and the burst went over Steve's head, burying itself in the sloping ceiling under the stairway.

Mungo lifted his head now to see what damage he had done, and when he glimpsed Steve coming up the stairs, he gave way to momentary panic, turned to run. Then he stopped short, with a nasty smile under his waxed moustache. He had just realized that neither Steve nor Johnny were shooting at him. And he was smart enough to understand why.

He turned around gloatingly, and pointed the weapon down at Steve.

"All right, you punks!" he snarled. "Take it now!"

Steve started to run up the remaining steps, and Johnny Kerrigan let out a roar of rage and sprang up after him.

Steve was only a third of the way up the flight, and Johnny just starting up. The muzzle of the Thompson was trained on them point-blank. Mungo couldn't miss. He waited just a fraction of a second, allowing Steve to get just a bit closer, but still not close enough. Then his finger began to tighten on the trip.

He should never have waited that fraction of a second. Because just as his finger began to grow taut, a grim and terrible figure appeared in the doorway of his own office, behind him.

It was the figure of Dan Murdoch.

Murdoch's face was set and grim, as he moved with all the lightning speed of which his long and supple body was capable. His arm snaked out and he smashed sideways with the edge of his open palm against the side of Mungo's neck. Mungo was sent staggering to the right, against the wall. Involuntarily his finger pulled the trip of the sub-machine gun, but Dan Murdoch had foreseen that. His other arm was already swinging up. It hit the barrel, sending it upward, and the short spray of lead beat a staccato tattoo upon the ceiling.

Mungo was snarling like a cornered beast now. He swung around, trying to level his weapon at Dan Murdoch.

But Steve Klaw was at the top. He hurled himself into Mungo, sending him crashing into Dan, who uppercut him beautifully. Mungo's head snapped hack, he let go of the Thompson.

Before he reached it, Murdoch caught him, holding him up, while Steve Klaw grabbed the sub-machine gun.

Johnny Kerrigan came storming up to the top, and patted Murdoch on the shoulder.

"How the hell did you get here?" Steve demanded. "I thought you were watching those bozos!"

Dan grinned sheepishly. "I got the itch to see what was going on, so I tapped them both on the bean and left them on the floor. When I got here I heard shooting, and people were streaming out through the front entrance, so I went around the back. There was an auto parked in the alley, and an open window above it. So I climbed to the car's roof, and in through the window, and what do I see but this ginzo about to perform a major operation on you two dubs!"

Police sirens were shrieking in the distance.

"Let's go," said Johnny Kerrigan. "Don't forget we're only private citizens now. We'd have a lot of explaining to do to the police."

"What about him?" Dan asked, jerking his head down at the limp form of Kris Mungo.

"We'll take him along," Steve decided. "If we corral enough of these birds, we should piece together some dope on Considine."

"Let's go!" said Johnny. He stooped and hefted Mungo up over his shoulder, and the three of them trooped into Mungo's office. They climbed out of the window, landing on top of the car, which was still parked in the alley.

"We can't go out that way," Kerrigan said. "This alley runs down into the next street."

Steve was peering into the parked car. "Very nice of this gentleman, whoever he is," he said. "The ignition key is right here. Pile in, boys!"

CHAPTER 6
GUNS OF THE G-MEN

A T ELEVEN o'clock that evening, Mr. Humbert Considine had been very angry. By midnight, he was in a cold rage, ordering all his thugs and gunmen available out on the job of trapping this Stephen Klaw who seemed to be bent on muscling into the racket, single-handed. By one A.M. he was beginning to be a little worried. By two o'clock he was frenziedly anxious.

The reports coming in to him were increasingly bad. His two private killers, Mike Stich and Looney Platz, had gone to the Tamiami Hotel to lie in wait for this Stephen Klaw and bring him in. That was the last he had heard from them. Then the Sunset Club got the works, with the place in a shambles, and the police called in. It seemed from the reports, that this Klaw had been reinforced by a couple of other fire-eaters, and they had just taken the Sunset Club apart, and kidnaped Kris Mungo. Then these three had gone on a real tear, visiting another half-dozen Considine spots, and acting with their usual gentle savagery.

So by two o'clock in the morning Mr. Humbert Considine was beside himself with fear and anxiety. So far, almost twenty of his most vicious thugs were dead, wounded or missing. His night club spots were wrecked, and his slot-machines were a shambles. Desperately, he got his hat, left his apartment and drove in his big maroon limousine, across the County Causeway to police headquarters in Miami. Since he didn't have his two precious bodyguards with him—Mike and Looney having been sent out to trap Klaw—Considine had to content himself with two big .45 calibre revolvers, and his chauffeur.

At police headquarters he got out of his car and stormed into the office of Detective-Captain Schultz, who was in charge at night.

"By God, Schultz," he shouted, "I want some action. I want some protection. Are you going to let that Klaw and his hellions ruin my whole business?"

Captain Schultz didn't care much for Considine. But they had never been able to prove a crime against him, and as long as he was apparently an honest business man, he was entitled to courteous treatment by the police.

"I'm sorry, Mr. Considine," said Captain Schultz, barely repressing a smile at sight of the Big Boss's evident agitation. "But we've been doing everything in our power. We just don't seem able to catch up to those three hellions. They move too fast for us. I just got a report that they wrecked one of your places out on the Tamiami Trail. They must be plain crazy—or else they're the three bravest guys in the world. They walk into the toughest spots—and come out with whole skins. You'd think they were *begging* to get knocked off!"

Humbert Considine smashed a fist down on the captain's desk. "I want some action. I'll be ruined. Put police guards at all my places!"

Schultz looked at him sourly. "You know how we feel about slot-machines, Considine. I don't care if everyone of them gets smashed. And anyway, you never looked for police help before. You always seemed to have enough armed guards without the police. How come now?"

"Damn you, Schultz," barked Considine, "you'll be sorry for this. Don't forget I have plenty of influence. I make a big contribution to the campaign fund every year. I'll get the commissioner to come down on you like a ton of bricks!"

Captain Schultz shrugged. "In the meantime, it looks like these three troubleshooters have already come down on you like a ton of bricks."

"Who are they, anyway?" Considine demanded. "Have you any idea?"

"Well," said Captain Schultz judiciously, "there are a lot of rumors going around. Some say that those three are the advance guard of a big gang from the North that's getting ready to muscle into the rackets. Others say that they're G-men, tearing the town apart to find the killer of one of their boys. It seems a G-man was found dead up in Carolina, and they suspect he was killed down here. You wouldn't know anything about that, Mr. Considine—would you?"

Considine's face had become sphinx-like as Schultz talked.

"G-men?" he said queerly. "No. I don't know anything about that. Why should I?"

"Well, I don't know," Captain Schultz said innocently. "Only that G-man was thought to have been in the Sunset Club the night he was killed. Of course, all your boys deny having seen him, so I guess it was all a mistake. But I wouldn't want to have to convince those three devils. Their names are Kerrigan, and Murdoch and Klaw. The rumors say they are called the Suicide Squad, and they sure live up to their name."

"This is outrageous!" Considine shouted. "I'll telephone Washington at once, and have the F.B.I. order them back to Washington!"

"I'm afraid that won't help you, Mr. Considine." There was a twinkle in Schultz's eye. "You see, three men with those names resigned yesterday."

Considine stormed out of police headquarters, and climbed into his car. Peavey, the chauffeur, said, "Where to, Boss?"

"The Tamiami Hotel!" he snapped. "I want to see what's become of Mike and Looney!"

WHEN THEY pulled up in front of the Tamiami Hotel, Considine put a hand on one of his guns, and started to get out of the car. But just as he got the door open, a slim, wiry fellow who looked like a kid appeared from nowhere, and putting a hand on Considine's chest, shoved him back into the seat. Then the newcomer slipped in alongside him, and there were suddenly two automatics in his hands. One of the guns bored into Considine's ribs, the other pointed unwaveringly at the back of Peavey's head.

"Just keep on driving, Mr. Chauffeur," the newcomer said in a conversational tone of voice. "Or, if you prefer it, I'll shoot you in the back of the head, and take the wheel myself."

Peavey turned around, looked into the slate-grey eyes behind the gun, and gulped. "I'll drive," he said.

"Smart boy," approved Stephen Klaw. "Go down on Biscayne, and turn east to the Tamiami Trail. I'll tell you when to stop."

Humbert Considine stirred uneasily. "Look here," he said. "I guess you're that Stephen Klaw who's been wrecking my places. Now maybe we can talk business—"

"No," said Klaw. "We can't talk business."

Considine glanced at him sideways, as the limousine sped west on Flagler Street. "What's your object in all this?" he demanded. "If you're trying to muscle in for some out-of-town mob—"

"I'm not trying to muscle in," said Steve. He raised his voice a bit, talking to Peavey. "Swing south at the next corner. When you hit the Tamiami Trail, slow down."

Considine was surreptitiously wriggling the gun out of his left-hand pocket, which was on the other side from Steve. He got it almost all the way out, when Steve calmly leaned across him and hit his wrist hard with the barrel of the automatic.

Considine let the gun drop back in his pocket, and gasped with the pain of the blow.

"Damn you," he grated, "you'll go to jail for life for this. I'll get you—"

"You're not getting anybody," Steve told him. "You're through. You didn't know it, but you were through when you knocked off Tommy Grant."

Considine drew in his breath sharply, "Then you're a G-man!"

Steve didn't answer.

"Listen," Considine said desperately. "I swear to you I didn't have anything to with that—"

47

"Stop right here, Mr. Chauffeur," Stephen Klaw said, disregarding him entirely. "In front of this building."

The building was an old structure, low and rambling. Projecting from the front porch there was a sign which read:

WAYSIDE INN

"Say!" exclaimed Considine. "That's one of my places!"

"It *was,*" Steve corrected. "My friends and I have taken it over for tonight. We brought a few of *your* friends over."

He opened the door and stepped out, with his guns covering Peavey and Considine.

"All right," he said. "Last stop."

Stephen Klaw herded them inside at the point of his gun. The door was opened for them by Dan Murdoch, who smiled sourly when he saw Considine.

"Just in time to join the party," he said.

DAN LED them into the large dining-room, which occupied the front part of the building. At one end of the room the floor had been cleared of chairs and tables, and four men were lined up there, against the wall. Johnny Kerrigan was keeping watch on them, with the machine-gun which they had taken from Kris Mungo.

Considine's eyes narrowed as he noted who those four were. Two were the hoods whom Steve had brought up to his room for Dan to guard. Looney was the third, and Kris Mungo the fourth.

Stephen Klaw shoved Considine and Peavey over against the wall to join them.

"What—what are you going to do?" Considine asked.

Johnny Kerrigan got up from the chair in which he had been sitting, and raised the sub-machine gun to his shoulder.

"Say when, Steve," he said to Klaw.

Steve nodded. "I guess we're all set—"

"Wait!" cried Considine. He turned to look at the others in the line with him. They all seemed without hope. Kris Mungo looked crookedly at Considine. "It's curtains for us," he said. "These three guys are the Suicide Squad. They're gonna knock us off and take the rap for it."

Considine's face was white. "Wait! No! You can't do that. You can't slaughter us—"

"Did you ever hear of the Saint Valentine's Day Massacre?" Dan Murdoch asked. "It's going to be repeated now. You were all implicated in the murder of Tommy Grant. We can't prove it in court. But we know you six killed him. So we're paying off."

Looney, who was standing awkwardly with his wounded shoulder, said bitterly, "Well, you gotta learn how to take it in this racket. I told the boss not to burn that G-man."

Considine turned on him viciously. "Shut up, you fool. They won't go through with it. They're just trying to get us to talk!"

"That's partly right," said Stephen Klaw. "We'd rather have you talk. We'd rather see you convicted in court, and hang for it. But if you won't talk, then it's *this!*" He motioned to the machine-gun.

Kris Mungo wet his lips. "Listen," he said hoarsely. "Suppose a guy talked. Would he get a break?"

"*You* would," said Steve. "If you gave us enough to hang Considine."

49

"All right, then. I'll talk!"

Looney had been leaning weakly against the wall. He straightened up and lunged at Mungo. "You dirty rat—"

For a minute they were tangled, and Dan Murdoch jumped in to drag them apart. In the confusion, Considine yanked out his two .45 calibre revolvers, and started racing toward the rear of the dining-room.

Johnny raised the sub-machine gun, but he couldn't shoot, because the others were in the line of fire.

Considine reached the rear door, leading into the kitchen, but he didn't go through. Instead, he reached up and pulled the electric switch behind the door. The room was plunged in darkness.

Considine's guns began to spit flame into the room. He was firing viciously, indiscriminately, not caring whether he hit friend or foe.

In the darkness there were sounds of struggle as several of the men jumped Dan Murdoch, who was closest to them. Johnny Kerrigan swore softly, as he dropped the Thompson gun, and pitched into the fight in the darkness.

Only Stephen Klaw saw the opening at the back door, and guessed that Considine was slipping through to make good his escape. Klaw leaped after him, and orange flame spat out at him. The ball sang past his ear, and someone behind him cried out. He thought he recognized Looney's voice, but he didn't stop to find out who had been hit. He raced after Considine, plunging through the dark kitchen. He saw the back door open into the yard, and started to blaze away with his two automatics in answer to Considine's.

Steve ran through the hail of lead, and emerged into the yard. By the trickle of moonlight slanting across the yard, he saw Considine duck behind a row of beer barrels, and poke the .45s out at him.

Steve kept on running, and Considine shot hastily, frantically. The big guns bucked in his hands, throwing the shots high. He fired twice with each gun before Steve reached the barrels and leaped over them. Considine cried out in fright, and turned to run, but Klaw made a flying tackle and tripped him. The two of them sprawled on the ground, as Considine brought up a knee to Steve's groin. Steve sensed the blow coming, and twisted over on his side, and the knee caught him in the hip.

Considine tried to bring his guns to bear on Steve, but Steve smashed him in the face with the barrel of one of the automatics.

He felt bone crunch under the blow, Considine whimpered, and covered his face. "I quit!" he cried.

STEVE DRAGGED him up by the collar, back into the dining-room. The lights were on again. One of the two hoods was lying dead on the floor, and Looney was bleeding from a high stomach wound.

Dan Murdoch said, "Considine's bullet got him."

Kris Mungo, Peavey, and the other hood were standing against the wall again with their hands high in the air.

Steve shoved Considine into a chair. The slot-machine king had his face covered with both hands, and a trickle of blood was seeping through.

"My nose!" he moaned.

Steve paid him no attention. He joined Dan Murdoch, who was kneeling beside the dying Looney.

Looney looked up at them, and his lips tried to form words. The effort was terrible to see. His face was beaded with sweat. He was holding both hands against his stomach.

"I… guess… I'm done!" he managed to get out. "Considine shot me… didn't care who he… killed. Rat."

"Will you sign a statement?" Stephen Klaw asked.

Looney's lips twisted into a ghastly smile. "You told me… I'd be a… rat. You were right. Get… me a priest!"

AN HOUR later, they had Looney's deathbed confession, and a signed statement from Kris Mungo and from Peavey, who had also decided to climb on the bandwagon. They saw Considine led away to jail, and Captain Schultz came over and grinned at them.

"There are a lot of charges against you boys, especially Klaw. But I guess it was all in the line of duty. You were G-men, and you were after a murderer—"

"Wait a minute," said Stephen Klaw. "We're not G-men. We resigned—"

Captain Schultz grinned broadly. "That's what I thought, too. But I was just on the phone, talking to your Director. He says he knows nothing about any resignations. He says you were on duty, and that you're to report back to Washington at once."

"Gypped!" said Johnny Kerrigan. "The Chief tore up those resignations on us. And I was looking forward to nine-days' vacation before going back!"

COFFINS FOR
THE SUICIDE SQUAD

CHAPTER 1
VOLUNTEERS TO DIE!

S TEPHEN KLAW'S train arrived in New York at 8:55 P.M. He slipped quietly off it.

Walking through Pennsylvania Station, his slim and wiry figure might have been mistaken for that of a kid back home from college for the holidays—were it not for those cold, slate-grey eyes of his, and for the sure and effortless way in which he handled himself.

He kept both hands dug deep in his overcoat pockets as a flock of newspaper reporters and cameramen surrounded him.

"Is it true, Mr. Klaw, that you've been sent here to hunt down Dunstan Vardis?"

"That's true," said Steve. "Dunstan Vardis escaped from Leavenworth five years ago. Since then he's made a business of harboring wanted criminals. He controls the most vicious gang in the country."

"Are you going to capture him dead or alive?"

"Either way."

"Suppose he gets you first, Mr. Klaw?"

Steve shrugged. "I'm paid to take chances."

"What about the Suicide Squad?" one of the reporters

Just as this moment
the gun went empty.

persisted. "Where are your two partners—Johnny Kerrigan and Dan Murdoch?"

Klaw shook his head. "That's their business. Now, if you'll excuse me—"

"Just a minute, Mr. Klaw!" a photographer begged. "Stand still for a second, will you?"

The man raised a bulky camera to his eye and sighted through the periscope. He had his finger on the lever to click it down. Before he could do so, Stephen Klaw took his right hand from his pocket. There was an automatic in it. Without wasting a fraction of an inch of motion, Klaw fired from the hip.

The shot echoed and re-echoed like thunder in the vaulted train-shed. The slug smashed square into the camera, driving through the box and embedding itself in the photographer's skull. The man went hurtling back, and at the same time there was an explosion from the camera.

Flame lanced upward from it and a bullet screamed wildly into the air, thudding against the steel arch far overhead. Had the camera been pointing at Stephen Klaw, the bullet would have hit him between the eyes.

Those two almost simultaneous shots created a veritable inferno of panic in the great railroad station. Stephen Klaw slipped the automatic back in his pocket, and stepped over to the side of the dead man. A couple of the reporters, with eyes gleaming with delight at such a story, knelt with him. Flashlight bulbs exploded by the dozen.

"What a story!" exclaimed Kearney, of the World. He put a

hand on Klaw's shoulder. "How did you know he had a gun in that camera?"

Klaw pointed to the smashed box. Where the lens should have been, there was the round bore of a long-barrelled forty-five calibre revolver.

"Did you ever see a camera with a gun-muzzle for a lens?" he asked.

Police were surrounding them now, and it was necessary to clear a space around the body. Lieutenant Schirmer, of the Homicide Squad, took Steve aside.

"Do you think that man was an agent of Dunstan Vardis?" he asked.

Klaw stared at him without blinking. "What do you think?"

Schirmer scowled. "I think you ought to have a bodyguard. Are you crazy, Klaw? The F.B.I. has kept sending men in here one after the other, to get Dunstan Vardis. And Vardis gets them, one by one. He'll get you, too."

"Thanks for the tip," Steve said coldly.

Lieutenant Schirmer flushed. "Now get me right, Klaw. Nobody wants to see Dunstan Vardis laid by the heels more than I do. But the New York police department has been working on the case for a year. You G-Men think you can come in and clean it up in a month. You don't work right, either. You've got to play with stoolies, and keep your ear to the ground for information, and wait for a chance to grab him."

"That's not the way I do it," Stephen Klaw said. "I've been sent to get Vardis—and that's what I'm going to do."

Lieutenant Schirmer shrugged. "Have it your way, Klaw. I've

heard a lot about you, and those other two fellows, Kerrigan and Murdoch. You three are supposed to be the Suicide Squad of the F.B.I. Well, if you want to commit suicide, go right ahead. Should you get in a jam, call on me—if you have the time."

"Thanks," said Stephen Klaw. He nodded, and walked away.

As Schirmer watched him go, the Lieutenant's face was twisted into an expression of intense perplexity. He turned to one of the reporters who crowded around him.

"There goes a man," he said, "who isn't afraid of God or the Devil!"

WHEN STEPHEN KLAW got out into the street he turned north on Seventh Avenue, looking for a taxicab.

A girl in a sleek black Hudson seal coat came hurrying after him, with a handful of little ribbons attached to buttons. She had yellow hair, and deep blue eyes.

"Won't you buy a button, sir," she said, smiling, "to help the starving Chinese?"

Without giving him a chance to refuse, she came up close, and started to pin the button to his lapel. Her lips were still smiling, and she seemed to be saying something to him in a bantering manner. But her voice was suddenly deadly serious, and there was live terror in her eyes.

"For God's sake, be careful, Mr. Klaw!" she breathed. "You're being watched. Pretend to give me a coin!"

Steve studied her quizzically. He took his left hand out of his coat pocket and slipped it into his trousers pocket. He took out a quarter and handed it to her.

"Who are you?" he asked.

"Never mind who I am. If you want to find Dunstan Vardis, come to see me tomorrow at noon. The Hotel DeGrasse, Room 715. Ask for Miss Lee."

She slipped the quarter into a little tin box, and started to hurry away.

Stephen Klaw reached out and caught her wrist.

"Not so fast, Miss Lee," he said tightly. "It's too long to wait till tomorrow at noon. You tell me what you know—now!"

"Oh God," she groaned, "you mustn't. They—they'll see us talking."

"Who will see us talking?"

"Dunstan Vardis' men. Don't you understand? You're being watched every second!"

"Interesting!" said Klaw. He kept his grip on her wrist. His glance swept up and down the street. There were several men idling nearby, but there was nothing to indicate that they were the men of Dunstan Vardis. "How do you know we are being watched?"

She tried to drag her wrist away, but unsuccessfully. "Oh, you beast! I thought you were clever, and could help me. I—I'm sorry I approached you. Let me go quickly, before they shoot us to death!"

Stephen Klaw grinned thinly. "Let's see those buttons of yours!" He lifted up her hand, which was clutching the buttons with the colored ribbons attached. They were all green, but the one she had pinned on his lapel was red.

"So," he said, "you pinned this ribbon on me so that Dunstan Vardis' gunmen may recognize me later, when they come to

59

look for me. You were posted here for this purpose, in case that photographer failed!"

She ceased struggling. Her eyes met his. A faint, bitter smile tugged at her lips.

"Well," she said, "what are you going to do about it? Will you arrest me?"

"No. I couldn't prove that you work for Vardis. I'm going to let you go." He released his grip on her wrist. "Goodbye, Miss— Lee!"

She stared at him a moment, unbelieving. "You—you're taking that ribbon off?"

His eyes were cold and hard. "On the contrary, Miss Lee, I shall wear it. Go back and tell Dunstan Vardis that I shall wear it all the time—to make it easier for him to find me!"

The girl sucked in her breath sharply.

"Stephen Klaw," she said, "you are a very brave man!"

Then she turned and walked swiftly away.

Steve looked after her, fingering the ribbon in his buttonhole. Almost imperceptibly, he nodded in her direction.

Two men who were sitting in a sedan fifty feet back, saw that nod, and understood its meaning. One of them was big and blond, with the shoulders of a stevedore. The other was tall and slender and black-haired.

The black-haired one, at the wheel, said, "The Shrimp wants her tailed, Johnny. You take care of her, and I'll stick with him."

"Right," said Johnny Kerrigan.

He slipped out of the car, and moved leisurely off in the direction taken by the girl with the yellow hair. No one would have suspected that he was following her, or was even interested in her. But he would not lose that girl. For all his great stature and powerful build, there was not a better shadower in the F.B.I. than Johnny Kerrigan.

Stephen Klaw waited only till he was sure that Johnny had the girl in sight. Then he turned and flagged a cab, knowing that Dan Murdoch, in the F.B.I. sedan, would keep following on his tail.

THESE THREE men—Kerrigan and Murdoch and Klaw—worked together with the smooth efficiency of well-oiled machinery. All three of them were able to think fast on their feet. And what was more, they thought along the same lines—so that it was hardly ever necessary for them to hold prolonged conferences to decide on a course of action. Each knew that the other two would go through hell for him, and none of them ever had to doubt that the others would hesitate in the face of danger.

They were called the Suicide Squad. For in the F.B.I. they rated only those assignments from which there was little chance of returning alive. Originally, there had been five of them. Now there were only three. Tomorrow, there might be only coffins for the Suicide Squad. But that was the way that Kerrigan and Murdoch and Klaw wanted it. Hard-bitten, headstrong and wilful by nature, they could not have brooked a life of routine investigations and patient trailings of minor bank defaulters or absconders.

And this was the job they had wanted. The name of Dunstan Vardis had become almost legendary in the underworld since his escape from Leavenworth five years ago. In some secret and mysterious way he had developed a sure-fire method of hiding wanted criminals. Every killer in the underworld came to Dunstan Vardis for protection. Convicted murderers with money could pay Dunstan Vardis to effect their escape. Trigger-men and dope smugglers paid Dunstan Vardis a percentage of their regular take as insurance against the time when they might be captured. And in this way Vardis had built up an organization powerful enough to make itself felt in every field of crime. So strong had Dunstan Vardis become, that he felt himself ready to challenge the F.B.I.

Three young Special Agents had already paid the price of attempting to track him down. Yesterday, young Lawrence had been found with his eyes gouged out. They hadn't killed the young Special Agent. They had blinded him.

Almost on the heels of that, in the early hours of the morning, another agent—Jack Sloan—had met death, his body hurtling down through space from the fifteenth floor of an office building where he had gone to make a routine investigation which must have uncovered something about Dunstan Vardis.

So when the Director of the F.B.I. had called Kerrigan and Murdoch and Klaw into his office, they were eager to come to grips with Dunstan Vardis.

Stephen Klaw's eyes had been grey and cold. "Tony Lawrence was blinded unnecessarily," he said harshly. "The kid couldn't have been dangerous to Dunstan Vardis. Why, he was just breaking in. He was only assigned to investigate the relatives of fugitives!"

The Director nodded somberly. "That's true of Jack Sloan, too. It looks as if Dunstan Vardis is throwing down a challenge to the F.B.I. If he can do things like these, and go scot free, then the underworld will figure him invincible, and they'll accept him as their undisputed leader. He'll be the King of Crime, from coast to coast!"

"Do we get the assignment, sir?" Klaw asked grimly.

"Yes. We won't handle it through the New York office, and we can't send a big force of men in there. There isn't enough to work on. It will be up to you three to stir things up, so that Vardis will come out in the open—give us some leverage, so to speak."

Dan Murdoch's dark eyes were frosty. "We'll stir things up, all right!"

"There's only one tangible thing for you to work on," the Director continued. "It may be the break we need. A girl named Nina Prentice phoned direct to this office from New York. She talked to me personally. She's the sister of Gerald Prentice. Remember him?"

All three of them nodded.

"Prentice," said Johnny Kerrigan, who had a prodigious memory for names and faces, "was convicted of diamond smuggling. He drew five to ten in Leavenworth. He escaped a year ago, and a guard was killed. The death of the guard has been published, but not connected with Prentice's escape, so that he won't know he's wanted for murder. It's strongly suspected that Prentice's escape was planned by Dunstan Vardis."

"Right," said the Director. "Well, Nina Prentice phoned that she has information for us. I've arranged for one of you to meet her secretly in New York. She's frightened stiff that something may happen to her brother, and she insists on going through a lot of rigmarole to keep the meeting secret. It may be worth it. I'll give you all the information before you start. Now, how are you three going to operate?"

"As usual, sir," Klaw said promptly, "I'll go in alone. We'll let them know I'm coming, and just when. Maybe Dunstan Vardis will make a try at me." He grinned thinly. "That would be very helpful. Johnny and Dan will work in the background."

The Director shook hands with all three of them. "Take care of yourselves," he said earnestly. "Don't take too many unnecessary chances."

And so here they were in New York. And Dunstan Vardis had already made a try, and failed. And it was certain that he would try again—and again.

CHAPTER 2
KILLER IN A DERBY

KLAW TOOK a cab to Forty-Second Street and Fifth Avenue. He did not look back once, confident that Dan Murdoch was there, behind him. If he were being tailed, Murdoch would know it, and would know how to deal with the shadowers. It was important now that Stephen Klaw should not be observed for the next ten minutes.

He paid off the cab at the Forty-Second Street entrance of the Public Library, and walked swiftly up the steps. In the hall, he stopped to look at a bulletin board, and saw that a short, squat man in a derby hat had just come in after him, and had paused and bent down as if to tie a shoelace. Steve's eyes flicked to the doorway, and he saw the tall figure of handsome Dan Murdoch entering the building.

Murdoch's eyes met his for an instant, and flickered. Then he nodded toward the squat man in the derby, who still seemed deeply interested in his shoelace.

Stephen Klaw smiled, and turned away from the bulletin board. He cut across the corridor toward the elevator, and saw the squat man get up from tying his shoelace, and start after him. But the man had taken only two steps before Steve heard Dan Murdoch's voice raised: "Say, mister! You dropped this ten dollar bill!"

Klaw kept going. When he reached the elevator he did not enter it, but went around it into the rear hall. He followed this hall around, and it brought him out back again into the front lobby, near the bulletin board. He just caught a glimpse of the squat man hurrying down the cross corridor, with a ten dollar bill clutched in his hand. Murdoch was grinning after him.

At the cost of ten dollars, Dan had held the man up long enough for Steve to lose him.

The man would undoubtedly think that his quarry had gone up in the elevator to the main reading room on the third floor, and would lose valuable time in looking for him up there.

Steve turned and went in through the large double doors opening into the ground floor Circulation Room. He glanced at his watch, comparing it with the clock there. It was exactly nine-thirty. He was on time to the minute. He went past the librarian's desk, and turned into the end lane of bookshelves, containing scientific books.

A slim young woman with dark hair was examining a book. The fingers with which she turned the pages were long, slender, patrician. She looked up quickly as Steve entered the aisle, and then looked down.

Klaw stopped quite near her, and looked at the book in the top shelf. This section, the little placard at the top of the shelf announced, was devoted to Science—Criminology. At once, Steve found the book he sought—Abingdon's Anatomy of the Criminal.

He took it from the shelf ostentatiously, and opened it to the title page, holding it in such a way that the dark-haired girl could see it. She drew in her breath sharply. In turn, she flipped the pages of her book back, so that her title page was visible. It was, "Modern Criminal Investigation."

At once, Steve smiled. "Miss Prentice?" he asked.

Her eyes widened with a sudden flicker of relief. "Mr. Klaw?"

He nodded, showing her his identification card case.

Her hands were shaking with excitement as she put her book back on the shelf. "Thank God you made it! I—I was afraid they'd get you before you left the station!"

"Thanks to your warning, I was on guard," Steve told her. "And now, talk quickly. There's very little time. You told our Director over the phone that you had information about Dunstan Vardis?"

"Yes. But I'm afraid it's not very much. You—you know all about my brother, of course?" she whispered shakily.

Steve nodded. "Your brother, Gerald Prentice, was arrested for smuggling uncut diamonds from Holland. He swore he was framed, but he was convicted by a Federal Jury and sentenced to five years in Leavenworth. He escaped. He is still a fugitive from justice."

"That's true," she said in a low voice. "You have the facts. But you don't know the—the terrible truth behind them. Gerald could have cleared himself by naming a certain woman. He didn't, because he loves her. He took his punishment to protect her. Gerald is innocent. He has a large income. He didn't need to smuggle diamonds."

"What has all that got to do with Dunstan Vardis?" Stephen Klaw asked impatiently.

"I'll tell you," she said. "The woman who framed Gerald is called Zara. She works for Dunstan Vardis. It was a scheme to get a hold over Gerald. It was Dunstan Vardis who helped him escape from Leavenworth."

STEVE WAS watching her closely, watching the swift play of emotion across her sensitive features. "You have proof of this?"

She dropped her eyes. "No. But I've seen Gerald twice since he escaped. I'm going to see him again tonight. I—I'll turn him over to you!"

Steve's eyes narrowed. "You'll betray your own brother? Why?"

"Because otherwise, I'm sure he'll be killed. Dunstan Vardis is using him. He's promised to help Gerald escape from the country through the underground channels he controls. But I'm sure he intends to kill him. I—I've talked to Dunstan Vardis. The man is all evil!"

"All right, then," said Steve.

"No. Wait. There's a condition. You must promise something first. I understand the F.B.I. can't make bargains with wanted men. But you—you have leeway. Don't turn Gerald in. Hold him somewhere. If, within forty-eight hours, you are able to catch Dunstan Vardis, you must promise to release my brother. *I'll help you catch Vardis!*"

For a long minute, Steve studied her carefully. "I'm sorry," he said at last. "I can't do it."

"But why?" She put a hand earnestly on his arm. "What good would it do to put Gerald in prison? His crime was only smuggling—even if he wasn't framed."

"You're mistaken," he told her harshly. "When Gerald Prentice escaped from Leavenworth, one of the guards tracking him was shot and killed. That makes it murder!"

Nina Prentice's eyes snapped wide open. Her face became utterly white. "Murder! But that's impossible! Gerald never told me. Nothing was ever said in the papers."

Stephen Klaw's voice became a little more gentle. "The murder of that guard was not made public until two days later. And it was made to appear in the newspapers as if it had no connection with your brother's escape. You see, we were sure even then, that Dunstan Vardis had helped Gerald escape. We weren't laying all our cards on the table at once."

"Then—then—" she was very plainly struggling to make herself realize the full meaning of what she had just heard Gerald faces the gallows if he's captured?"

Klaw nodded soberly. "The gallows. Or life imprisonment at

best. Do you still want to turn him over to me? Though perhaps, if you aid in the capture of Dunstan Vardis, the court will take that into consideration. His sentence might be commuted—"

"No, no. Better let Gerald take his chance with Vardis. Maybe I'm mistaken. Maybe Vardis doesn't intend to kill him."

Steve shrugged. "As you please. Technically, I should take you into custody, since you admit having information about Vardis. But I'm not going to do it. Should you decide to play ball with us, call me at the Hotel Montrose."

He stopped quickly, for Nina Prentice uttered a short cry. He saw her eyes fill with terror as she looked over his shoulder.

"That man! That's Joslin! He'll tell Vardis I was talking with you. They'll surely kill Gerald."

STEPHEN KLAW had already swung around. He caught a glimpse of the squat man in the derby hat, whom he had eluded in the lobby. The man had evidently come around the back way after him. He was looking at them now with a triumphant leer. He turned away swiftly.

"Oh, God, stop him!" Nina Prentice exclaimed in a tense whisper. If he tells Dunstan Vardis—"

She had no time to finish. Suddenly, Dan Murdoch appeared in the aisle. The squat man recoiled as he came face to face with Dan.

Murdoch put a hand on his shoulder. "Not going yet?" he asked pleasantly.

The man jumped back, and his hand flew to a shoulder holster. It came out with a gun.

Dan Murdoch clucked his tongue. "Not in the library!" He

stepped in with a swift, lithe motion, bringing his fist up in a short, beautiful arc that landed flush on the fellow's chin. The man tumbled backward along the aisle, into Stephen Klaw's arms.

Steve grasped his wrist, and twisted. The man gasped with pain, and let go of the revolver. Dan Murdoch stepped in and caught it before it struck the floor. Then Stephen Klaw let go of the wrist.

Their teamwork had been so swift and efficient that the man was disarmed before he knew what was happening to him. Nina Prentice stared at them, a hand pressing hard against her breast. She had never seen two men act so swiftly and in such perfect unison.

Klaw winked at her, and swung the man around. "Well, Mr. Joslin," he said, "what do you think we ought to do with you?"

Joslin stood tense, between Dan and Steve. "I ain't talkin'," he said.

Dan Murdoch shook his head deprecatingly. "Too bad," he murmured. "You're under arrest."

"What for? You ain't got a thing on me."

"What about this gun?" Steve asked.

Joslin looked at him slyly. "Okay, but that's state law. You got to turn me over to the cops."

Nina Prentice said breathlessly, "If you turn him over to the police, he'll get a lawyer. Vardis has several lawyers who appear for his gunmen when they're in trouble. Joslin will tell that he saw me talking to you, and Dunstan Vardis will surely kill Gerald!"

70

Stephen Klaw raised his eyebrows. Joslin smirked. "I don't know what you're talking about. I never heard of Dunstan Vardis."

"See," said Steve. "He's a perfectly innocent man. He was only carrying the gun for protection against bookworms in the library."

"In that case," said Dan Murdoch, "I guess we'll have to let you go. Scram."

"No, no!" exclaimed Nina. "You mustn't—" But she stopped at a wink from Steve.

"We're not holding you," Dan Murdoch told him. "You claim we haven't a thing on you. So get going."

Joslin looked a little surprised, but quickly he gained confidence. He started to squeeze past Dan Murdoch.

Dan took out his revolver, and spun the cylinder. Stephen Klaw took out one of his automatics. For a brief moment they looked at each other very seriously.

"Who gives it to him, Shrimp," Murdoch asked. "You or I?"

"You take him, Dan," Steve said. "You have a new gun. You want a chance to try it out."

Joslin drew in his breath sharply. "What—what you guys gonna do? What—what you gonna do with the gun?"

"Get going!" Dan said implacably.

"You're gonna shoot me down!" Joslin exclaimed. "You're gonna shoot me when I go down the aisle. That's it! You're gonna shoot me, an' you'll say I resisted arrest!"

"Well," said Dan, "what did you think we were going to do?

Hurry up—" he gave the man a little shove—"let's get it over with!"

"Wait!" Joslin begged. "For God's sake, wait. You can't kill me like this."

"No?" Murdoch asked softly, looking down at him out of slitted eyes.

"I'll talk!" Joslin blurted. Terror had complete hold of him now. "I'll talk! I'll tell you anything you want to know. But don't kill me!"

"WHERE CAN we find Dunstan Vardis?" Stephen Klaw demanded.

"I don't know!" Joslin breathed. "I swear I don't know. He gives me orders on the telephone."

"How do you report to him?"

"I wait for a call."

"Suppose it's an emergency?"

"Then I phone that woman—Zara. The one with the yellow hair."

Stephen Klaw's eyes gleamed. "The number?"

"Trafalgar 4-6047."

Nina Prentice said tensed, "That's the woman—Zara. The one who framed Gerald!"

"Nice work," said Dan, marking down the number Joslin had given them. He looked at Steve. "What do we do now, Shrimp?"

Steve grinned at him. "Just what you're thinking of doing, Dan. We'll call on Zara. I know where she lives. I'm pretty sure it's the Hotel DeGrasse. Joslin hasn't told us anything we didn't know. But he may come in handy. Let's go."

Dan Murdoch took Joslin's arm, and thrust him down along the aisle.

"Where you takin' me?" Joslin demanded.

Dan gave him a grin. "You've admitted working for Dunstan Vardis. That puts you in our jurisdiction, my friend. We're taking you up to the New York Field Office of the F.B.I. And if Vardis or anybody else can get to talk with you before tomorrow, then I'm a lame duck!"

They walked him out to the street between them. He was surly and resentful, sensing that he had been tricked into talking too much. Now it was too late. They had every right to hold him on a Federal charge after what he had told them. Murdoch handcuffed him, and shoved him in the car.

Steve took him aside for a moment. "You better stay at the Montrose from now on, Dan—in case Johnny phones in. I'll call you if the going gets hot."

Murdoch nodded, grumbling. "Now don't try to grab all the fun, Shrimp. If you try to cut me and Johnny out of it, we'll saw your ears off!"

"Don't worry," Steve told him. "I'll call." He watched Murdoch drive away, then turned to Nina Prentice. "Well," he asked, "have you made up your mind? Are you going to play ball with me?"

"Yes!" she said suddenly. "I'm going to trust my brother's life in your hands—even if you do promise nothing. The last two times that I met Gerald, it was in the basement of the Silver Galleon. That's where I'm to meet him again tonight. It's a night club downtown in the Village. The owner is a cripple named Farney. He never gets out of his wheel chair, and he seldom shows himself. He opened the Silver Galleon about a year ago, and it has become a hangout for the underworld."

"What time are you supposed to be there?"

"At midnight. I'm to sit at one of the tables. The last two times, a man came and took me to an inside room. Then he blindfolded me, and led me through a lot of passages. When the blindfold was removed I was in a room with Gerald. There weren't any windows in the room. Gerald said he himself didn't know where he was. They had blindfolded him, too. They were waiting for a chance to smuggle him out of the country."

Steve was listening carefully. "All right. Be there at midnight, just as if nothing had happened. I'll be there, too. Don't give any sign that you know me."

There was a trace of moisture in her eyes as she looked at him. "God help me, Stephen Klaw, I hope I'm doing right!"

CHAPTER 3
DEATH WEARS A MUFF

WHEN KLAW left Nina Prentice, he walked two blocks west to Times Square, fingering the red ribbon in his buttonhole. He crossed Times Square diagonally, and entered Emlen's Bar just off Broadway.

The place was busy. Thirty or forty people were seated around the horseshoe bar. Emlen's had long been a rendezvous for the tougher elements of New York's underworld. Crack trigger-men, mobsters on the loose, policy racketeers and dope salesmen congregated here. The sole requisite was that they should not be wanted by the police at the moment.

Stephen Klaw made his way to an empty spot at the bar, and seated himself on a stool. The man at his left glanced at him carelessly, and then stiffened. His eyes focussed on the red ribbon in Klaw's buttonhole. The man hurriedly downed his drink, left a coin on the bar, and went out.

Steve smiled. He slipped his right hand into his overcoat pocket. He saw the eyes of other people around the bar fixed on that ribbon. A couple of other men got up and left.

The bartender did not notice the sudden exodus. He moved over in front of Steve, wiping the bar. He started to say, "What'll it be, mis—"

He stopped short, breaking the word off in the middle. He had looked up from the bar. His eyes met Steve's, and he froze.

"Steve!" he choked.

"Hello, Mike," Steve said genially. "What's eating you?"

He knew Mike Emlen. A long time ago he had done Emlen a big favor. It had concerned Emlen's son, who was in a jam. Steve had helped the boy out of his trouble, at considerable risk to himself. Emlen had never forgotten it.

"Are you crazy, Steve?" he demanded hoarsely. "Don't you know that the word has gone out all over town to get you? Dunstan Vardis offers twenty grand to any torpedo who knocks you off!"

"Interesting," said Steve. "I'm glad to hear that Vardis puts such a high value on me."

"See here, Steve," Mike Emlen said earnestly. "I know you're tough. You've bucked pretty bad outfits in the past. But this is different. You can't beat Dunstan Vardis. Look how the bar is emptying. Some of these guys are stoolies for Vardis. By this time, they're phoning him that Stephen Klaw is in Mike Emlen's with a red ribbon in his buttonhole. They'll be coming for you. And you can't fight a whole mob single-handed."

"How do you know I'm singlehanded?"

"I know how you work. When the Bureau sends you, they don't use a regiment. At the most, you've got Kerrigan and Murdoch. Three men. Against maybe a couple of hundred. Vardis is a big man, Steve. He's got every torpedo in town eating out of his hand. They give him a cut of every job they do, just for protection. He's got a system of some kind, for helping them to escape if they get caught. He smuggles them out of the country in some way."

"I know all that, Mike," Steve said wearily. "I thought maybe you could give me some new dope."

"That's all I know—except that you'll be dead in less than twenty minutes if you don't get under cover."

"Do you know about a place called the Silver Galleon?"

Mike nodded, looking around at the quickly emptying bar. "Yes. The Silver Galleon is a joint down in the Village. It's owned by a cripple named Farney. Nobody knows where Farney came from. But he has plenty of dough. Some say he fronts for Dunstan Vardis." Mike kept wiping the bar in front of Stephen Klaw. "And now, why don't you take a tip from a guy who means well by you, Steve. Get out of here. Don't try to take Dunstan Vardis singlehanded."

"What about this woman that's called Zara?" Steve persisted.

"She's pure poison!" Mike Emlen told him. "She's dangerous because she's got looks and brains. To look at her you'd think she was an angel. But inside, she's worse than a snake." Emlen broke off sharply, sucking in his breath. His eyes were fastened on the entrance. "Speak of the devil—"

STEPHEN KLAW had kept an eye on the door all the time that he talked to Emlen. He saw her as soon as Mike did. It was Zara, the yellow-haired woman whom he had met a short time ago.

She stood for just an instant, inside the doorway. She was no longer wearing the Hudson seal coat. Now she had a tawny nutria coat, with one of those fashionable little hand-muffs to match it. Both her hands were in the muff as she moved grace-fully up to the bar, alongside of Klaw. She did not smile. She seemed to be studying him, as if he were some new kind of being she had never seen before.

She didn't spare a single glance for Mike Emlen, who moved discreetly out of earshot. Fully three-quarters of the patrons had already deserted the place. Those who remained were on the far side of the bar away from where Klaw stood.

Zara leaned against the bar, facing him. Her glance nicked down to the red ribbon in Steve's buttonhole.

"A little while ago, Stephen Klaw," she said, "I told you that you were a very brave man. Now I must tell you that I think you are a fool."

Klaw's eyes nickered. "Is that your own opinion? Or is it a message from Dunstan Vardis?"

"Take it any way you wish." She moved a bit closer to him. "I like you, Stephen Klaw. That's why I came to warn you. You are doing a very foolish thing. You have nothing to gain by allowing yourself to be killed by the gunmen of Dunstan Vardis. Why do you expose yourself this way?"

Steve's face was inscrutable. "I appreciate your interest, Zara. Did you come to warn me because you like me—or because Dunstan Vardis is worried about what my two partners are doing? Is he afraid that Kerrigan and Murdoch are somewhere around?"

Zara smiled ruefully. "You're a hard man, aren't you, Stephen Klaw? You trust no one."

"Yes," he said, "There are people I do trust. But you aren't one of them. Go back and tell Dunstan Vardis that he doesn't have to worry. I'm alone here. Kerrigan and Murdoch aren't anywhere around. He can safely send his gunmen."

"Why?" she insisted. "Why do you challenge him like this?"

He smiled tightly. "I'm going to break down the reputation of Dunstan Vardis, my dear Zara. I'm going to show the rats of the underworld that he isn't invincible. I'm going to show them that one man—not the whole F.B.I., but just one man—can take everything that Dunstan Vardis can hand out, and still come back fighting. I intend to show the underworld that its idol has feet of clay!"

Zara sighed. "It's a pity, Stephen Klaw. You're the kind of man I admire. It's too bad you have to die!"

SHE STIFFENED, and her elbows pressed close against her sides. The little nutria muff pushed out, against Steve's stomach. He read in her eyes what she was going to do. There was a gun in that muff. She was going to pull the trigger, and send a slug into his stomach. The fur would kill the sound of the explosion. She would turn and calmly walk out, as he slumped down to the floor.

"Don't do it, Zara," he said, in a low, conversational voice.

She paused for a fraction of a second, her eyes questioning.

"As you see," he explained softly, "my right arm is resting on the bar. As you can also see, my left hand is in my coat pocket. Do you know what it's doing there? It's holding a thirty-two calibre automatic pistol. The muzzle is pointing at your beautiful body. If you shoot, Zara, I shoot, too. It would be a shame for one as beautiful as you to die-now!"

Mike Emlen had said that she was like a snake, inside. For an instant, her deep, innocent blue eyes seemed to change color, and to glitter with a tinge of reptilian green. But immediately she veiled them. When she looked at him again, that glitter was gone, and she was smiling.

"I was mistaken, Stephen Klaw," she murmured. "I said that you were a foolish man. You are not. You are a very clever man—and still a very brave one. I shall go now. Tell me—would you shoot a woman in the back?"

"No," he said. "Go and tell Dunstan Vardis not to send a woman to do a man's job. Ask him why he doesn't come himself!"

Zara raised her eyebrows. "Do you want me to admit that I know Dunstan Vardis—so that you can arrest me?"

He shook his head. "I could arrest you, if I wanted to, for violating the Sullivan law. I'm sure you don't have a permit for that gun in your muff. But I'm saving you till I can arrest you for murder. Take a tip from me, Zara, if you had anything to do with the killing of Tony Lawrence, or Jack Sloan, or the other G-Men who were sent after Dunstan Vardis, then be sure not to be around when the blow-off comes. I'll have no mercy for you."

She was smiling no longer. The fierce intensity of his voice had shaken her. She turned around very slowly, and walked out into the street.

Stephen Klaw watched the door close behind her. He couldn't see her outside, because the Venetian blinds over the windows were all the way down. But he didn't take his hand out of his pocket.

"Make it Scotch," he said to Mike Emlen, who had come up alongside him.

He drank it neat, without a chaser, not noticing that it came out of a bottle that was Mike's private stock—a Scotch that can't be bought any more, since the war began.

He took out a bill and laid it on the counter, but Mike Emlen pushed it back into his hand. "I'm not taking your money, Steve," he said.

Klaw nodded his thanks, and took the money back. Then, with both hands in his pockets, he went toward the door.

"Good luck, Stephen Klaw!" Mike Emlen called after him, softly.

CHAPTER 4
LIGHTNING WAR

A S STEPHEN KLAW stepped out of Mike Emlen's place, one question was beating like a hammer against his brain: *Where was Johnny Kerrigan?*

Johnny had set out to tail Zara. Surely, if nothing had happened to him, he would have followed her inside. If Johnny had given up the trail of Zara, it was either because he had been killed, or because he had come across a hot lead to Dunstan Vardis. In the latter case, he might have left a message at the Montrose Hotel, which they had agreed upon beforehand as their contact point. He started for the Montrose, which was only two blocks away.

There was no sign of Zara. She hadn't lingered after coming out of Emlen's.

Klaw walked warily now, watchful of everything and everyone in the crowded street. From now on it was certain that Dunstan Vardis would wage a *blitzkrieg*. For Vardis must know that a challenge had been thrown down to him which all of the underworld could understand. One man was challenging him. Or, let us say, three men. Dunstan Vardis had planned for a big war—a war with the whole F.B.I. Certainly he must have expected that when his operations became known, the whole weight of the Federal Bureau of Investigation would crack down upon him. He had convinced his followers that he had a strong enough organization to win against the nation's great crime-fighting bureau. What now would those followers say if they saw that only three members of that Bureau had been assigned to the task of ferreting him out? And what would they say when they saw that those three lone men were checkmating their clever and ruthless boss?

The psychology of the Director's tactics was perfect. But the Suicide Squad would have to bear the brunt of an attack which had been planned for an even larger force.

Stephen Klaw understood all this as he walked toward the Montrose Hotel.

Now that Zara had failed in her treacherous attempt at Klaw's life, Dunstan Vardis might be expected to stage more spectacular attempts. Machine-gunning in the street? A bomb? A dope-crazed murderer? He had used all these methods before, and no doubt had ample facilities for using them again. Klaw therefore, walked warily.

By the time he reached the Montrose Hotel, he knew definitely that he was being followed. There were at least two men on foot, behind him, whom he had spotted. And there was a Black and Gold taxi which was also most certainly tailing him. It kept crawling a half block in back of him, and never gaining.

Three times Stephen Klaw stopped and went to the curb, where he would afford a tempting target for anyone in the cab. Each time, he kept his hands in his overcoat pockets, and watched the two pedestrian tailers out of the corner of his eye, as well as the cab. If it should start to gather speed to come shooting past him, he would be prepared.

But they failed to rise to the bait. Each time that he stopped, they stopped. Evidently, they had something else planned—

something that would be more certain of obtaining the desired result. Or else they were waiting to choose the most favorable spot for the attack.

With narrowed eyes, Klaw continued up Broadway, then turned west to the Montrose Hotel, which was in the middle of the block.

Then they struck.

It was typical of Dunstan Vardis, that the attack was different from anything that might have been expected.

Stephen Klaw grasped the idea at once. And too late, he understood how clever was his adversary.

THREE DRUNKS had been staggering A down the street from the Montrose Hotel, toward Steve. Two other men, standing near the curb, were arguing loudly about something or other. Steve suddenly discovered that all these men were clustering closely around him. At the same time, the two tailers came hurrying up from behind, and joined the press of men closing in on him. The Black and Gold taxi accelerated and pulled up alongside at the curb.

None of the men had guns in their hands. They just closed in, purposefully, grimly. The pseudo-drunks were still making noise, talking and laughing loudly. But their eyes were on Klaw. They pushed in so close that his elbows were pinned to his sides.

Simultaneously, someone opened the door of the taxicab, and it yawned invitingly. The close-pressed group of men began to surge toward that open door, half pushing and half carrying Klaw with them.

"Don't get tough!" one of the men said. "Dunstan Vardis wants to see you. Better get in the cab without scrap-ping!"

Steve braced himself, and pushed against the crushing weight of the close-knit group.

"Okay," one of them said. "He's gonna make trouble. Sap him!"

Blackjacks appeared in several hands. They rose to slam down upon Steve's skull.

Klaw sighed. "Sorry, boys," he said. And he fired both automatics through the cloth of his pockets.

He fired four times with each gun, and the noise of the blasts was almost smothered by the close-pressed bodies. The slugs struck his assailants low, mostly in the groin, for they were fired at hip-height.

Blackjacks fell from nerveless hands. Men screamed in awful agony. They fell away from him as if they were puppets whose strings had been cut. Those who were not hit, turned and ran in sudden, frantic terror. The wounded men writhed on the sidewalk at Steve's feet. The taxi motor roared, and the cab sped away, with open door swinging wide. Men and women pedestrians rushed headlong away from the vicinity, anxious to get out of range.

Stephen Klaw did not spare a single glance for the wounded men on the sidewalk. He kept his hands on the guns in his pockets, and stepped away from the writhing mass. Black, scorched tears showed in the cloth of his overcoat as he walked toward the Montrose Hotel.

He could have stopped and waited for the police, and participated in questioning the wounded men. But he had no time. He must find Johnny Kerrigan and Dan Murdoch, and he must be in the Silver Galleon at midnight. He was sure that little information about Dunstan Vardis could be gleaned from those men. Like Joslin, they probably knew nothing about their boss. He must be content now with his temporary victory.

A moment after he stepped away from that spot, he was only one of the hundreds of pedestrians on the crowded street. It was night, and the passers-by were panic-stricken by the sudden shooting. It was certain that none would be able to point him out to the cop who was running up from the corner with drawn gun.

Quietly, Stephen Klaw turned in toward the entrance of the Montrose Hotel.

But he had hardly taken a step toward the entrance, when a woman screamed, across the street.

Klaw's eyes swiveled toward that long drawn-out shriek of terror. He saw the woman, standing transfixed, pointing frantically toward an upper window of the Montrose Hotel.

KLAW WAS already under the canopy of the hotel entrance. He was not in a position to see what was happening above the canopy. But his instincts were those of a fighting man, always attuned to danger. Especially now, when he knew he was at war with the cleverest and most ruthless enemy the Suicide Squad had ever encountered.

Almost in the same split-instant that he saw the woman, he saw other people on the opposite side of the street looking upward and gesticulating wildly. He needed no more than that.

He went into a flying leap that carried him forward, to land flat on his face on the sidewalk, just past the canopy.

Almost simultaneously there was a ripping, rending sound. A heavy armchair tore through the canopy, tearing the canvas as if it had been paper, and twisting the iron framework into a mass of curlicued wreckage. It crashed to the pavement with the force of a projectile, and disintegrated into a thousand catapulting splinters.

For an instant, everything was silent in that street. It was as if the whole world had stopped moving. Even the screaming woman had ceased to scream. Then, abruptly, the spell was broken. The woman on the opposite side of the street found her breath again. Hysterical shrieks poured from her throat.

The cop, who had reached the group of wounded men, was uncertain whether to remain with them or to come and investigate this new phenomenon. A man shouted, pointing upward, "That chair came from the fifteenth floor!"

Someone else yelled, "No! I saw it. It was pushed out of the tenth floor!"

A milling mass of people began to swirl around in the gutter, blocking off all traffic. People began to argue and gesticulate. A small crowd gathered around the wounded gunmen. Even for jaded New Yorkers, this combination of a gunfight and a huge chair hurtling out of a window, all within the space of two or three minutes, was too much. Pandemonium swept the crowd in no time.

In all the excitement, they lost sight of the central figure— the one at whom all this had been aimed, Stephen Klaw was no longer there. Unobserved, he had sprung to his feet and hurried into the hotel.

Grimly, he pushed through the revolving doors into the lobby. Dunstan Vardis had first tried to capture him alive. Then, failing that, he had made an immediate attempt to kill him.

Klaw understood very well why Vardis wanted him alive. He wanted information about Kerrigan and Murdoch. Perhaps he had planned to torture it out of Klaw. He wanted to eliminate all three members of the Suicide Squad. He would probably have left Stephen Klaw to be found in some dark street, with his eyes gouged out, like Tony Lawrence. But Vardis, like a good general, had figured on possible failure. He had prepared a quick second attempt. And he would keep on trying. For now it was becoming vital to Dunstan Vardis that he dispose quickly of the Suicide Squad. His vicious prestige was at stake.

The clock over the clerk's desk in the lobby showed that it was twenty minutes before twelve. Little enough time to get down to the Silver Galleon by midnight.

People were streaming out of the lobby, brushing past Steve, almost bowling him over in their eagerness to get outside and see what had happened. He pushed through them toward the elevator. The indicator was in motion, moving past the third floor. By the time he reached the door, the indicator showed that the cage was at the main floor. The door began to slide open.

KLAW KEPT his hands on the two automatics. It was possible that the men who had thrown that chair were coming down to make their escape. They could easily walk out of the hotel unmolested, for no one could prove who had sent the chair hurtling out of the window. In fact, it would take some time to discover the window from which it had come.

Klaw watched with narrowed eyes as the door slid fully open. The operator stood aside, and three men came out.

Klaw's glance slid past them, and his eyes gleamed as he saw who was standing far back in the interior of the cage. It was Dan Murdoch. Dan must have been upstairs in their room, and had sprinted for the elevator at the first sounds from outside.

Steve had only a second to exchange glances with Murdoch. The three men who had emerged from the elevator suddenly stopped, staring at the red ribbon in Steve's buttonhole.

"That's him!" one of the three shouted. They all made concerted jabs toward their shoulder holsters.

Stephen Klaw stood very still, a set-hard smile on his lips, his agate eyes inscrutable, his hands deep in his pockets. He was waiting for them to get their guns out. He had no need to shoot. Dan Murdoch stepped lithely out of the cage, directly behind them.

"As you were, gentlemen!" he said pleasantly. And suddenly there were guns in Murdoch's hands, boring into the backs of the two men on the ends.

Those two stiffened, with their hands actually touching the butts of the guns in their shoulder holsters, but not daring to draw them. The one in the middle, however, felt no muzzle at his back. His lips drew back from his teeth in a snarl. Whirling, he yanked out his gun.

Stephen Klaw shot him as he turned—through the head. He fired from the right hand pocket, and at the same time his left hand automatic came out to help cover the other two. They stood stiff as soldiers on parade, never moving a muscle, as their companion stretched both hands over his head, then collapsed crumpling to the floor at their feet.

The single gunshot reverberated through the lobby, but there was no one to see what was happening. Everyone had run out into the street. Only the elevator operator watched them, his mouth agape.

"Nice work, Shrimp," said Dan Murdoch approvingly. "I wish I could shoot from my pocket the way you do!"

He had not moved, keeping the two guns boring into the prisoners' backs.

"What'll we do with these rats?" he demanded. "They're the ones that shoved the chair down on you. I was looking out the window, and I saw them do it."

"Upstairs," said Steve.

The two gunmen allowed themselves to be herded into the elevator. The operator sent the cage up to the tenth, and their room. Once in the room, they swiftly disarmed the thugs, and handcuffed them to the radiator.

"What about Johnny?" Steve asked anxiously while they worked over the two gunmen. Any word from him?"

"Nothing!" Murdoch told him. "He didn't call in. Maybe he's still on the girl's tail."

"He isn't," said Steve. "I met her. Johnny was nowhere in sight."

"By God," said Dan Murdoch, "if anything's happened to Johnny, I'll take Mr. Dunstan Vardis apart, piece by piece."

He turned and glared at the two handcuffed prisoners. They cowered at what they saw in his eyes. But Dan Murdoch immediately recovered his self-control.

"Don't go away, boys," he urged them. "We'll be wanting a few words with you, by-and-by!"

Murdoch and Klaw went down in the elevator, and the operator goggled when they showed him their F.B.I. badges.

"Let us out at the basement," Klaw ordered him. "We have no time to stop and answer questions. After we've gone, get hold of Lieutenant Schirmer of the Homicide Squad. He should be around somewhere. Tell him to go up to our room and ask those boys a few questions."

"Y-yes, sir!" the operator stuttered.

"And tell him," Klaw threw back as they stepped out of the cage, "that the Suicide Squad is still alive and kicking!"

Under his breath he added, so that only Dan Murdoch could hear, "*I hope!*"

They were both thinking of Johnny Kerrigan as they got into the car, which Murdoch had parked around the corner on Eighth Avenue. They went roaring downtown, utterly disregarding traffic lights, and police whistles.

"It's seven minutes of twelve," Steve said. "We've got to get there by midnight. I don't want Nina Prentice to be alone in the Silver Galleon for a minute!"

CHAPTER 5
THE KILLER ORDERS EGGS

THEY MADE it, just as the bells of Saint Mary's Church were tolling midnight.

The Silver Galleon occupied a brownstone house just across the street from the waterfront, at the edge of Greenwich Village. Opposite, was a row of abandoned warehouses, formerly used by the Jersey Shore railroads, but long since condemned. Beyond the warehouses was the river, with the riding lights of half a dozen yachts, and the tall superstructure of a heavy cruiser visible against the Jersey shoreline.

Stephen Klaw left Dan Murdoch, and went directly into the main entrance of the Silver Galleon. Strains of an orchestra came wafting out as the doorman opened the door for him. Within, the smell of stale spaghetti permeated the tobacco-laden air.

A girl at the coat room tried to take his overcoat, but he shook her off. She started to argue with him, insisting that no one could go in without checking his hat and coat, but she stopped with her mouth open, staring at the red ribbon in his buttonhole. She said not another word, but scurried off down a narrow hallway.

Klaw grinned twistedly. The warning was given. In a moment every killer in the place would know that Stephen Klaw was here for a showdown.

A headwaiter came to him, out of the crowded dining room. The man had a barrel chest, and big, hairy hands. He looked out of place in a waiter's outfit. He would have been more at home, wielding an iron bar or a blackjack in some strikebreaking fracas. His eyes rested on Klaw for a moment, and Steve saw him purse his lips as he spotted the red ribbon.

"You alone, mister?" he demanded.

"Yes."

"Okay. Right this way."

He started to lead Klaw to a table in the center of the room, but Klaw stopped him. "I'll take that table—over near the wall," he said.

"That's reserved, mister. You got to take what you get, in here."

The headwaiter found himself talking to thin air. Steve had already started for the table near the wall. The bruiser cursed under his breath, and took a quick, angry step after Steve. He put out a big hamlike hand to grasp his shoulder. But Stephen Klaw seemed to have eyes in the back of his head. He turned just at the right moment, and his cold, level, eyes met those of the bruiser.

"Never try to put a hand on me!" Klaw said softly. He had both his own hands in his overcoat pockets.

The headwaiter jerked his fist back, as if he had touched fire. "Okay, okay, mister. But I tell you that table is reserved—"

"Cancel the reservation, then!"

Klaw crossed the room, passing between aisles of tables whose occupants stared up at him and his ribbon with hard, appraising eyes. There was no doubt in his mind now that Nina Prentice had been right when she said that this place was the hangout of Dunstan Vardis' paid killers. He seated himself at the table he had chosen, pushing his chair around so that his back was to the wall. The headwaiter stood irresolute, a few feet away, wondering how to handle him.

Steve paid the man no attention. He let his gaze wander over the room. An orchestra was chopping out indifferent music, and fifteen or twenty couples were moving slowly around on the roped-off square in the center. His eyes flickered as he spotted Nina Prentice.

She was seated alone at a table alongside the dance floor. Her long, sensitive fingers were wrapped around the stem of a cocktail glass, but she hadn't touched its contents. She was staring off into space, as if studiously trying to avoid seeing Stephen Klaw.

OUT OF the corner of his eye, Steve saw Dan Murdoch come into the room. The headwaiter went over to greet him. Evidently no one in the place recognized Murdoch as one of the Suicide Squad. That was all to the good.

Murdoch waved the headwaiter away, and instead of taking a table he went over to the bar at the other end of the room, and stood with his elbows on the railing, facing the floor. Over his shoulder he ordered a drink from the bartender.

The orchestra ceased playing, and the couples went back to their tables. Now, a dozen more pairs of eyes became focussed on Steve, as word went around to those who had just finished dancing that Killer Klaw was here in the place.

Steve saw the attention he was attracting, and smiled thinly. A waiter came over to him to get his order.

"I don't want a thing," he said to the man. "Just go and tell Dunstan Vardis that Stephen Klaw has come for him!"

The waiter tried to look innocent. "Dunstan Vardis? I never heard the name."

"Then you ought to read the newspapers," Klaw told him. "On second thought, never mind taking the message. Vardis surely knows it by this time. You might tell him, though, that if he doesn't come out in ten minutes, I'm going to start taking this place apart—to see what's behind the false front!"

The man flushed, and hurried away.

Klaw half-closed his eyes, as if he were dozing. But his head was thrown back, so he could see everybody in the room. Suddenly he stiffened. He almost lost his pose of easy somnolence. He blinked, and looked again. Yes, there could be no doubt about it—*the man in the waiter's uniform, who had just come out of the kitchen, was Johnny Kerrigan!*

Steve felt a surge of gladness. He had been sure, for the past hour, that something had happened to Johnny. He looked across to the bar, and saw that Dan Murdoch had also spotted their big partner.

Johnny was carrying a tray with two sandwiches, which he served to a couple at a nearby table. Then he started back to the kitchen. He threw a quick side glance at Steve, and nodded his head almost imperceptibly.

Steve caught his cue. "Waiter!" he shouted imperiously, raising his hand.

Johnny turned, apparently saw that he was wanted, and came over to Steve's table. Steve picked up a menu, and pretended to be asking him about the food. In reality, he said swiftly, "What's the lay, Johnny?"

94

Kerrigan bent over him, as if advising on the dishes.

"This is it, Shrimp!" he said. "This is Dunstan Vardis' head-quarters. I followed that dame down here. She went in the front entrance, and I could see her talking to a cripple in a wheel chair, in the foyer. I decided to take a look around the back. The place wasn't open for business yet, so I broke into the cellar and looked around. There's a secret passage of some sort that leads under the street to those warehouses on the waterfront. I came upstairs, and what do I do, but run into that cripple in the wheel chair, with four or five hard guys. I was just going for my gun, when the cripple says: 'Oh! You're the waiter the Acme Agency sent!' I said yes, and that's how I'm a waiter. But I got no gun. I heard the cripple telling one of the boys to frisk me, so I ditched my gun in a big pot of soup. Now I can't get it."

"Take one of mine," said Steve softly.

"Nix. Too dangerous. We're probably being watched. That cripple—Farney—has a million eyes. What are you and Dan doing here, Shrimp?"

"We're going to work in about ten minutes, Johnny. It's the showdown."

"Okay. I'll change to my street clothes, and work my way down to the cellar. I'll see can I get through that underground passage to the warehouse. If you get that far, come through after me."

"Right, Mope."

"Right, Shrimp. See you in hell. If no see no more, say good-bye to Dan for me."

With that, Johnny Kerrigan turned away and headed for the

kitchen, writing down an imaginary order for a chicken liver omelette.

BARELY A moment after Johnny Kerrigan had disappeared into the kitchen, Stephen Klaw was treated to another surprise. A door opened in the wall, close to where he was sitting. The yellow-haired woman, Zara, came into the room. She was clad in a daring, low-cut evening dress which was molded to every curve of her voluptuous body.

She threw a quick side-glance at Stephen Klaw, but did not greet him. Instead, she walked right past him, and went over to the table where Nina Prentice was sitting. She bent low, with her back to Steve, and talked swiftly with Nina. Then Nina arose, her face flushed with clashing emotions, and followed Zara back toward the side door.

Immediately, Steve was alert. Zara was taking Nina Prentice to see her brother. And he had reason to believe that Nina would never come back from that interview. Dunstan Vardis could not afford to leave Nina alive, to tell what she knew. He was going to cause her to disappear.

As the two women approached the door, Stephen Klaw got up from the table, and signalled with his hand across the room to Dan Murdoch. Then he stepped directly in the path of Nina and Zara.

The yellow-haired woman looked at him coldly. "What do you want, Stephen Klaw?"

He smiled. "Nothing, dear lady—except to go along with you and Miss Prentice."

Zara shook her head, her eyes never leaving his. "No, Stephen Klaw. You see—here, *I* am the mistress!"

She must have given some secret signal. For now, a group of men were pushing close around them, coming from the nearby tables. Their hostility was no longer veiled. They had guns in their hands, and the guns were covering Stephen Klaw from a dozen angles. Two of the men stepped deftly in front of Zara, so that their bodies shielded her from Klaw's guns. The others moved in close to him, from all sides.

Klaw smiled, keeping his hands in his pockets. "Very neat, my dear Zara. You deliberately brought Miss Prentice this way, to get me away from the table—so I wouldn't have a wall at my back."

"Thank you," Zara acknowledged. She took Nina Prentice by the arm, and dragged her around behind the screening bodies of her gunmen.

"Finish him without noise if you can!" she ordered. "Have the orchestra play loud music."

She stopped, her face becoming paper-white. Her hand dropped from Nina Prentice's arm. Behind her, Dan Murdoch had suddenly appeared. He was pressing the muzzle of his revolver to the white skin at the back of her neck.

"I think," he drawled, "that I have the situation well in hand, Shrimp. The lady understands that as soon as these rats of hers fire the first shot, I'll fire the second—into her pretty spine!"

Zara stood motionless. Her eyes blazed with fierce hatred at Stephen Klaw. "What do you want?" she demanded hoarsely.

Steve stepped back, pushing the gunmen out of his way. As

long as their mistress was threatened by Dan Murdoch's gun, they didn't dare resist.

Klaw reached behind him, and opened the door in the wall. He stood to one side, and bowed. "Ladies first!" he said.

Zara stepped forward unwillingly, with Dan Murdoch close behind her. Nina Prentice followed them through.

Stephen Klaw remained where he was. "Keep going, Dan," he called out. "I'll be along in a couple of minutes."

He closed the door behind him, and stood with his back to it, facing the roomful of gunmen. His hands came swiftly out of his pockets, gripping the automatics. The room had become so still that the snick of his safety catches was distinctly heard.

"All right, boys," he said softly. "Come and take Killer Klaw!"

CHAPTER 6
DEAD END FOR G-MEN

FOR THIRTY tense seconds, there was not the slightest movement in all that room. Men with guns in their hands were facing Stephen Klaw—men as hard-bitten as any to be found in the underworld. They had only to press the triggers of their guns. But they remained unmoving.

Every one of these men had heard the almost legendary stories about the Suicide Squad. They had heard how Kerrigan and Murdoch and Klaw had gone into dens where they were outnumbered ten to one—and had come out alive. They had heard how the three hellions of the Suicide Squad seemed actually to *seek* death—and yet, never to find it. Just now, these gunmen had been ready, hot for a fight, under the eye of their mistress. That had been due to the desire to shine before her. There was no doubt that she commanded the unholy love of men, just as in the case of Gerald Prentice, who had been willing to allow himself to be framed into prison rather than betray her.

But now she was gone, and they knew that one of the terrible Suicide Squad had taken her away. Perhaps she would never return. What was the use then, of fighting this other one, who stood there so coolly, with his guns ready to blast? Some of them must surely die if a fight started.

Klaw could read these thoughts in their faces. He knew also, that their respect for Dunstan Vardis had perceptibly diminished in the past few hours. They did not have the blind confidence in him that had carried them on before the Suicide Squad appeared on the scene. They were not sure that Vardis could do the things for them that they had thought he could.

Time passed in that room, with each second ticking slowly, like an aeon of time. If only one of those men should decide to shoot, that would be the end of Stephen Klaw. He would go down, taking with him many of these rats. But he would be dead.

He faced the prospect calmly, without a flicker of emotion showing in his cold features. The men before him saw in him the modern incarnation of the flaming warrior of olden days, who wasn't afraid to die because he saw visions of Valhalla.

To them it was incomprehensible. These men killed for profit, or to save their skins. They didn't fight for the love of fighting, but to make a mean living. They could not understand one who offered to risk his life for honor, or for the love of battle.

Slowly, as the seconds ticked away, some of the crowd at the back of the room started to trickle out, slinking away and hoping that the hard-eyed man with the automatics would not notice them.

STEPHEN KLAW saw them steal away. And he let them go. He faced those others nearest him, and a little smile of contempt twitched at his lips, for he saw that they would not fight.

"All right," he said harshly. "Listen to me, all of you. As I look at your faces I don't see any who are wanted for serious crimes. Perhaps the wanted men are in some other part of the building. You are all *would-be* gunmen and thugs. You haven't the guts for a real fight. You thought you'd have an easy time of it under the protection of Dunstan Vardis. You even thought that with Vardis behind you, you could laugh in the faces of the G-Men. Well, I'm a G-Man. Let's see which of you wants to laugh first!"

There was no response. Indeed, many of them looked away from him, lest he think they were defying him.

It was Stephen Klaw who laughed at last.

"Get out! All of you!" he ordered harshly. "Get out of here, and leave town. Never come back. Dunstan Vardis won't be able to help you after tonight. Leave your guns. And never try to make a living by guns again, because you'll surely come up against the G-Men, and next time you may not be so lucky!"

Uncompromising and unsmiling, he stood there with his automatics, and waited.

He had not long to wait. Almost before he had finished talking, men began to stoop and lay their guns carefully on the floor, and quietly slink away. Soon there was no one in the great room, except Stephen Klaw. He raised one hand, and wiped sweat from his forehead. Then he turned, and opened the door in the wall. He went through into the passage, after Murdoch.

There was a dim bulb illuminating the hall. He followed the corridor to the end, with his automatics out. He came to a flight of stairs leading down. At the foot of the stairs he saw an open door. The door was in a larger hall, and he saw that the hall led on beyond that open door, seemingly into utter darkness. Klaw did not follow it any farther than the door. He stepped through it into a small room.

Murdoch was there, and Zara, and Nina Prentice. Murdoch still had his gun in Zara's back. But none of them was looking toward the door. None of them saw Stephen Klaw enter.

They were too busy looking at that which was at the other end of the room.

THERE WAS an opening in the far wall, where a sliding secret door had been opened, affording a view of another dark passageway beyond. But framed in that opening there was a grotesque and revolting man.

He was seated in a wheel chair, which could be propelled by a self-contained motor. The lower half of the man's body was covered by a robe, and only his head and torso were visible. His head was tremendous. It was shaped like an egg, and the narrow chin served all the more to accentuate the unbelievable width of his skull. His forehead was shining white, like wax, and he wore a wig which was so manifestly not his natural hair that one wondered why he bothered to wear it at all.

This queer creature was chuckling. And the chuckle made a

101

horrid, vile sound in the room. The reason for his amusement was the Thompson sub-machine gun which lay across his lap, pointing at Murdoch and the two women.

"Well, my dear friends," he was saying, "it seems that I shall have one last pleasure before leaving—the pleasure of raking you all with snub-nosed slugs! You and your two friends, my dear Murdoch, are entitled to my compliments. I never thought that the efforts of three men could break up the power of Dunstan Vardis!"

Stephen Klaw was invisible to the cripple in the wheel chair, because he had the darkness of the hallway behind him, and because Murdoch and the two women were between him and the open panel. He could barely see the man over Nina Prentice's shoulder. His eyes reflected puzzlement. This man was surely not Dunstan Vardis. He had pictures of Vardis, before the man had escaped from Leavenworth. There was not the slightest resemblance. This must be the cripple, Farney, who had been mentioned both by Nina Prentice and by Johnny Kerrigan. Yet he spoke as if he were the master.

And now, for the first time, Stephen Klaw saw that there was another man in the room. He was standing over at the left of Murdoch, and his hands were bound behind his back. His clothes were disheveled, and his hair was mottled. He lacked a shave, and there was blood on the right side of his face which had evidently trickled down from a wound in the scalp. But Steve recognized him at once. The resemblance to Nina Prentice was so marked that there was no doubt he was Gerald Prentice.

Prentice spoke now, for the first time. "Why kill my sister?" he demanded hoarsely. "Let her go, Vardis. She never harmed you."

The man in the wheel chair shook his head, still chuckling. "Impossible, my dear Gerald. You see, when I leave this place, I intend that none shall remain alive to say what Dunstan Vardis looks like." His eyes swung to Zara. "Not even you, my dear Zara!"

And then, he must have pressed some secret spring. For with the swift smoothness of a well-oiled mechanism, the secret door slid shut with a *click*. Dunstan Vardis disappeared, and nothing was left but blank wall. There was only one little aperture in that blank wall—a loophole. And now, the barrel of the submachine gun was thrust out through that loophole.

THERE WOULD never have been time for any of them to escape from the room before the gun began to stutter its flaming death. Zara screamed, and leaped to one side. As if her scream had attracted the killer's attention to her, the barrel of the gun swung in her direction, and flame streaked from the muzzle. The snub-nosed bullets lanced out at Zara.

But someone uttered a hoarse shout. It was Gerald Prentice. Shouting, he leaped forward awkwardly, in spite of his bound hands. And he threw himself directly in the path of that stream of lead directed at Zara!

Nina Prentice screamed as she saw his body battered by the flailing bullets. For a moment he danced in the air, as shot after shot thudded into him. Prentice was dead before he hit the floor.

But his sacrifice had been unavailing. For one single bullet had caught the beautiful Zara in the throat, and she fell slowly,

graceful even in death, upon the body of the man who had sacri-
ficed everything for her sake.

Dan Murdoch had thrust Nina Prentice behind him when the
machine-gun began its chatter. He raised his revolver, and fired
six times, quickly, straight at the bit of muzzle which showed
through the loophole. At the same time, Stephen Klaw's two
guns were spitting fire, at the same target.

Klaw fired seven times with each gun, emptying the clips.
He hit it fourteen times, and Murdoch hit it six times. Those
twenty sledge-like impacts in split-second succession must have
paralyzed Dunstan Vardis' hand, for the muzzle of the machine-
gun disappeared.

Klaw's fingers flew as he inserted another clip, and emptied it
into the blank wall. But none of his shots pierced it. The bullets
ricochetted into the room. That sliding door was made of sheet
steel.

They heard a sudden whining of machinery from behind the
door, and Klaw exclaimed, "That's an elevator, Dan! He's going
down!"

The two men swung out of the room, dragging Nina Prentice with them.

"Wait!" she begged. "Let me stay here. My brother—"

Dan Murdoch and Stephen Klaw looked at her with sympa-
thy. Murdoch patted her on the shoulder.

"Sure, kid. Stay with him. And don't feel too bad. Your brother
was a brave man. I'd have been proud to shake his hand."

There were tears of gratitude in her eyes for those few words
as she watched them hurry out. Then she turned to her dead....

KLAW AND Murdoch followed the long hallway, reloading as they went. They noticed that the corridor sloped downhill, and they guessed that it would lead them into the lower part of the warehouse fronting on the river.

"Johnny is down there!" Klaw said. "He said he was going down to look around. He'll run right into Vardis and whatever is left of his crew—and he hasn't got a gun!"

There were no lights here. The corridor was in utter darkness, and Murdoch used his flashlight. They came to a strong, oaken door, and stopped before it. Klaw tried the knob. It was not locked. He had his hand on the knob when he heard sudden shouts from the other side, sounds of a furious struggle.

"Let's go!" he shouted to Dan Murdoch.

He thrust the door wide open. They stepped through, shoulder to shoulder.

They were at the head of a flight of stairs, leading down into the basement of the warehouse. And this, they saw at a glance, was the final hideout of Dunstan Vardis. It was equipped like an arsenal. It was here that were stored the weapons used by Vardis' gunmen.

But they spared not a second glance for all that. Their eyes swept to the panorama of struggle in the center of the room.

Johnny Kerrigan was there. From somewhere he had gotten a gun and was fighting with it. But at just this moment it went empty. A dozen thugs were coming at him, and at the far end, where a sliding garage door opened out to the dock, sat the cripple in the wheel chair. He must have come straight down in the elevator. His face was twisted with rage as he urged the killers to close in on Johnny Kerrigan. For the moment, their guns were useless against him, for he seized one of their number and whirled him high above his head. He was using the inert man's body as a club.

Only Johnny Kerrigan, with his stevedore shoulders and his primordial strength, could have done that. He was flailing that body around, and the thugs were backing away from him, waiting for a chance to get in a shot.

As Murdoch and Klaw came down the stairs, Johnny swung the body, hitting two of the thugs. They went down like ninepins, and Johnny laughed out loud, deep in his chest, and went in at the others, not the least concerned about their guns.

A little rat-faced thug sneaked around in back of him, and raised his gun to deliver the killing shot in Johnny's back.

Klaw and Murdoch took care of him. Their guns began to blast as they came down those stairs, shoulder to shoulder. The first to fall was the little rat who had tried to shoot Kerrigan in the back. Then they went down, one after the other, as thunder filled the underground room.

Taken by surprise, those gunmen had no stomach for this hot work, facing all three of the Suicide Squad. They turned to run, but saw at once that they couldn't beat the burning slugs from the avenging guns of the three G-Men.

"Don't shoot!" they shouted, almost in unison. And their hands went up in the air, guns clattering on the floor.

Only one man did not give up.

That was the cripple in the wheel chair. Dunstan Vardis raised his machine-gun, with his lips drawn back in the snarl

106

of one who hates all the world. He raised it to cover Klaw and Murdoch. Klaw fired at his head and Murdoch at his torso. Murdoch's bullet killed him.

Klaw's forehead puckered in puzzlement. He had seen his slug hit the man in the head, but it had not even jerked him back. It had seemed to carry away part of his scalp, but there was no blood.

But Dunstan Vardis was dead, and that was the thing that counted. They came all the way down the stairs, and Kerrigan wiped blood from his face, and grinned.

"Hi, punks," he said. "You didn't come any too soon!"

Stephen Klaw patted him on the back. "That was nice club-work, Johnny, I never saw you do that before."

HE STEPPED past them, and went over to the dead body of the cripple. He knelt beside him, and uttered a low whistle. Kerrigan and Murdoch came over, keeping an eye on the prisoners, although it was hardly necessary, for they had no more fight in them.

They looked down at the head of Dunstan Vardis.

"No wonder I didn't recognize him!" Stephen Klaw said. "That's all wax!"

Indeed, Vardis had built up for himself a head of wax upon his own. The broad forehead, the hydrocephalus skull, were all made of wax. Stripped away, it revealed the true features of Dunstan Vardis.

"That's why he didn't want anyone to remain alive," Dan Murdoch said. "I mean anyone who had seen him. He must have put in a lot of effort on this disguise, and he didn't want to have to change it!"

Stephen Klaw turned to Kerrigan. "What about you, Mope?" he asked. "How did you get down here?"

Johnny grinned. "I just wandered down, and fell into a beehive. But come here. Let me show you what I found!"

First they tied up the prisoners with strips of burlap sacking, and then Johnny led them into an adjoining room.

"Take a look!" he said.

A girl was lying unconscious on the floor. "That's Mary Lawrence," he explained. She's poor Tony Lawrence's sister. She came down here yesterday. It seems that Vardis phoned her and told her he had her brother, and she could save him by coming. Well, the poor girl came down, and they held her, figuring that if the F.B.I. tried to get after Vardis for blinding poor Tony Lawrence, they could threaten to do the same to her."

"Is this where you found her?" Steve demanded.

Johnny nodded. "I came down here, and broke into this room, in the dark, and heard her sobbing. She was tied up. I flashed my light, and untied her, and she started to tell me her story. She found out what happens to the criminals who paid Vardis to get them out of the country. Here are a couple who were supposed to leave today."

He led them to an open trapdoor a few feet away, and pointed down the opening.

Dan Murdoch uttered an exclamation. "Coffins!" he exclaimed.

"Sure," said Johnny. "And dead men in them. They're Vardis's clients. He helped them to escape, all right!"

"I'm sorry we shot him," Stephen Klaw said. "I would have liked to see him hang."

Johnny Kerrigan kicked a machine gun lying on the floor. "See this? It almost finished me. I found it, and figured I owned the place. And then, while Mary Lawrence was showing me the coffins, three hoods jumped us. I turned the machine gun on them, but the clip held all duds. It didn't shoot."

"My Gawd!" said Dan Murdoch. "What did you do?"

Johnny grinned as he knelt and took Mary Lawrence's head in his arms, and chafed her skin to revive her. "I threw the gun at them!"

He pointed to a small huddle of bodies over in a corner. "The boys thought they'd like to take me without noise, so they all jumped me. Too bad for them. That's where I got the "club" I was using in there."

Twenty minutes later, the place was flooded with police, and reporters. Klaw was giving interviews, while Johnny Kerrigan held Mary Lawrence's hand, and while Dan Murdoch talked earnestly with Nina Prentice.

Lieutenant Schirmer scowled, and drew Stephen Klaw aside.

"Looks like those two buddies of yours are mighty interested in the girls. What do you think?"

Stephen Klaw looked over at them, and made a wry face.

"Only till the next job," he told Schirmer. "The Suicide Squad can't afford to get tangled up with women—except at the other end of a gun!"

THE SUICIDE SQUAD—
DEAD OR ALIVE!

CHAPTER 1
THE CITY OF TERROR

O N OCTOBER 1, John Stafford, mayor of Hill City, was shot and instantly killed by a dope-crazed assassin named Dill.

The next in line for the mayoral job was Lawrence Hall, president of the City Council. But, for some unaccountable reason, Hall refused the honor. In order to avoid becoming mayor, he resigned from the City Council and left at once for Florida, taking his wife and son with him.

It now became the duty of Judge Samuel Rotherwell, chief justice of the Superior Court, to appoint someone to fill the unexpired term of the mayoralty until the next election. There were a number of substantial business men and civic leaders in Hill City whom Justice Rotherwell might have chosen. But to the amazement and consternation of everyone, he named— Hugo Bledd.

That was how the Era of Terror came to Hill City.

Hugo Bledd owned the Hill City Race Track. He was a disbarred lawyer who had dipped his fingers in almost every form of shady activity. He had been disbarred for conspiracy to help a notorious racketeer client defraud the government of two

Dan Murdoch was coolly picking

them off as they came up.

million dollars in income taxes. And when his racketeer client went to jail, Bledd had continued to manage the vast *sub rosa* enterprises of the Big Shot. Disbarment meant nothing to him, as long as he was able to keep out of jail.... And this was the man whom Justice Rotherwell appointed to be mayor of Hill City!

Naturally, there was a good deal of criticism. The editor of the morning Journal announced that he would ask the Governor to look into it. But that night, the editor of the Journal was accosted by a group of thugs, who beat him with a lead pipe and left him unconscious in the street. The same night, there where a dozen other assaults upon citizens who might have been expected to oppose the appointment.

Hugo Bledd was sworn in the next day. He demanded the immediate resignation of the police commissioner, as well as of all the other commissioners who had been appointed by the preceding mayor.

He also discharged a great number of the older policemen and detectives, claiming that the police department needed revamping.

Then there began an influx of strange and ugly looking men into Hill City. From all parts of the country they came—men with tight lips and killers' eyes, men with guns bulging under their armpits, men who had done time in all the major prisons. Before the city awoke to its peril, it was in the grip of as vicious a mob of storm troopers as had ever taken possession of a European land.

One of these new arrivals, a man named Rory Fenn, was appointed police commissioner. Fenn immediately swore in a hundred of the newly-arrived thugs as policemen and detectives, raising some of them to captains' and inspectors' rank over the heads of the old-timers on the force.

The next day, at the meeting of the City Council, a contingent of these uniformed thugs was present in the meeting room. Significantly also, seven of the thirty-nine councilmen were absent. Two of the seven were dead. The other five were in the hospital, so badly injured that they would not be able to leave their beds for weeks.

Little wonder, then, that those councilmen present quickly voted to pass all the measures submitted by Mayor Hugo Bledd. A tax was imposed on all business transactions in the city, as well as on all pay checks. The money derived from this tax was to be placed in a relief fund, to be administered by the Mayor. In addition, Mayor Bledd was given the power to create five hundred new appointive positions on the police force and in other city departments, the salaries to be fixed by himself.

By the time the Council meeting was over, absolute dictatorial powers had been voted to Hugo Bledd. His thugs, wearing their brand new police uniforms, began making the rounds of all the retail stores in the city, selling tickets for a mythical police ball, at ten dollars each. No one refused to buy.

As if by magic, gambling houses opened over night. Slot machines appeared in every store and hotel lobby. Bookmakers began to transact business openly. Night clubs advertised obscene burlesque entertainment. Beady-eyed, slick-haired men began to peddle marijuana cigarettes near the public schools.

A fortune began to pour into the private coffers of Hugo
Bledd and Associates.

SOME FEW citizens still dared to voice an objection. Among
these was Norton Gregg, district attorney of Hill County, who
was not an appointee of the mayor, but was an elected State
official. He drew up an indictment to present to the grand jury,
but Judge Rotherwell refused to allow him to present it. He
was blocked.

Angrily, he left Judge Rotherwell's chambers and hurried
to his office. He put through a long-distance call to Governor
Daniel Elsing at the State capitol.

"Dan," he exclaimed hotly, "you've got to do something. It—
it's fantastic, unbelievable. Bledd and his crew are looting the
city. They're making it the crime headquarters of the whole
country. You've got to stop it!"

"What do you want me to do, Norton?" Governor Elsing
asked.

"Declare martial law in Hill City!" District Attorney Gregg
exploded. "Send in the troops—"

"You know I can't do that," the governor interrupted, "unless
the request comes from the mayor."

"Well—well—" Gregg fumbled for ideas—"call a special
session of the Legislature to appoint an investigating committee."

"Sorry, Norton, I can't do that either. You forget that this State
has home rule. The demand for a special session has to come
from the local authorities."

District Attorney Gregg gripped the phone blindly. He ran

his free hand through his fast-graying hair. "Good Lord, Dan, there must be *something* we can do. The law is being violated every minute. And Rotherwell—I don't know what's come over him. He's as honest a judge as I've known, yet he blocks my every move!"

"Why don't you call the F.B.I.?" Governor Elsing suggested. "Perhaps they can find a way."

District Attorney Gregg's hands were trembling as he hung up. For a long time he sat staring blankly into space. Then he picked up the phone once more and said harshly, "National-5303!"

In a moment, he was talking with the director of the Federal Bureau of Investigation, of the United States Department of Justice.

He talked for twenty-five minutes. At the end of that time he sighed and said, "Then there's no legal way in which you can send Federal agents here to break this up?"

"I'm sorry," he heard the director say. "There is no evidence of violation of a federal law. But wait. There's one thing I may be able to do. I have three men in the department who work independently, on a roving assignment. I'll ask them if they'd be willing to accept a furlough and go into Hill City as private individuals. I'm almost sure they'd accept—they're that kind...."

District Attorney Gregg interrupted: "Good Lord, are you mad? Three men! What can three men do—"

He stopped as he heard the director's voice in bleak amusement. "You don't know these three men, Gregg. If they accept, they'll arrive in Hill City tomorrow, and contact you. Their names? *Kerrigan, Murdoch and Klaw!*"

SLIGHTLY BEWILDERED, Attorney Gregg put down the phone. He didn't know what to think. The names the F.B.I. director had mentioned meant nothing to him. He felt tired, beaten, let down. There was no place he could turn for help. Still, he'd keep on fighting....

The door of his office was thrust violently open, and four men entered. Their leader was a big, bull-necked man with a flat nose and a pair of mean and vicious eyes which looked out from under bushy, unkempt eyebrows. Gregg recognized him as Rory Fenn, the new police commissioner. The other three were in plain clothes, but they were wearing new badges pinned to the lapels of their coats. They were no more prepossessing than their commissioner. They were three of the thugs who had been appointed to police posts—Hugo Bledd's storm troopers.

None of the four said a word. But there was something ominous in the way they stared at District Attorney Gregg.

Slowly, Rory Fenn crossed the room to the desk. One of his men remained at the door. The other two came around the desk and stationed themselves on either side of Gregg's chair.

A little line of perspiration appeared upon Gregg's forehead.

"What do you want?" he asked hoarsely, looking up across the desk at Rory Fenn.

Fenn didn't reply at once. He glanced around the office, then his gaze returned to the gray-haired district attorney.

"Get up!" he said.

"See here, Fenn," Norton Gregg exclaimed indignantly, "you have no right to come in here with your bullies—"

Fenn said, "Shut up!"

He leaned across the desk, and a big, hairy hand came up in a swift, open-handed blow to the side of Gregg's face. The slap sounded like the crack of a whip.

Gregg was thrown sideways, almost off his chair, but the two thugs standing alongside him caught him under the arms and hauled him to his feet. They dragged him to the middle of the room, facing Fenn.

"You've been making a nuisance of yourself, Gregg," Fenn told him, in that cold, toneless voice of his. "Your switchboard operator just tipped us off that you called the boss G-man in Washington. Now we'll show you what we do with guys who make trouble for us."

He drove his fist into District Attorney Gregg's face. All the power of his beefy body was packed behind the blow.

Gregg's breath escaped in a rush as his head was snapped back. His nose began to bleed. He would have sagged to the floor but for the support of the two thugs.

Fenn reached out and took a grip on Gregg's gray hair with one hand, pulling his head up, then drove his fist once more into the hapless man's face. This time he split both the upper and the lower lip.

Gregg squirmed, trying to break loose from the two ruffians who held him, but he was like a child in their hands. They laughed at his feeble efforts, and held him up while Rory Fenn smashed blow after blow into his face, gashing his cheek, lacerating his lips, loosening teeth, flattening his nose. Soon, Gregg's face was unrecognizable, bloody and battered. Twice they stopped and threw water on him to revive him, then continued.

At last, Rory Fenn's lips twisted in a smile of satisfaction. Gregg was hanging limp between the two gunmen, and blood was dripping over his clothes, down to the floor. He was moaning feebly.

"All right," said Rory Fenn.

The two thugs dragged their victim back behind the desk, and dumped him into the chair. Fenn got more water from the cooler, and splashed it across his face.

GREGG RAISED his head groggily. His eyes were puffed. "You devils!" he muttered. "You'll go to jail for this!"

Fenn laughed. "What jail, Gregg? We run the jail—like we run the rest of the town. Nobody goes in that we don't put in. Get wise to yourself. You can't buck Hugo Bledd. What you just got is only a sample. You play ball with us, or we'll really go to work on you."

"Never!" exclaimed Gregg, through swollen lips. "You'd better kill me now. Because if you don't, I swear I'll get every one of you—"

Fenn's laughter shook the room. "You got a daughter, haven't you, Gregg?"

The district attorney's pain-wracked body stiffened.

"Susan! What—what about her?"

"How'd you like her to get a dose of what you just got?"

"No! God, no! You couldn't—"

"She's in jail, Gregg. We had her picked up on a charge of

reckless driving. There's two of my boys outside her cell right now. All I have to do is pick up the phone and say one word— and they go to work on her!"

"You devil!" Gregg shouted, and sprang up.

Fenn laughed and, with an open-handed blow, smashed him back into the chair. Grinning, Fenn reached for the phone.

"Wait!" Gregg screamed.

Fenn stopped, with his hand on the phone. "Well?"

The district attorney's face was ghastly, clotted with blood, and torn with anguish. "Don't—don't hurt her. I—I'll do anything you ask."

"That's better!" grunted Fenn. "You'll write an article for the paper, saying that you had no right to draw up that indictment. You'll say that Hugo Bledd is a fine mayor for Hill City, and you'll urge everybody to get behind him and support him. You'll say that hereafter, as district attorney, you will vigorously prosecute anyone who attempts to oppose Mayor Bledd.... And you'll write it now."

Slowly, with trembling hands, District Attorney Norton Gregg took paper and pen and began to write. He was a beaten and broken man.

"You—you'll not hurt Susan?" he begged.

"Not if you do what you're told," Fenn assured him.

When Gregg had finished, Fenn took the paper and put it in his pocket.

"Now," he said, "pick up that phone and call the F.B.I. Tell 'em to forget the whole thing. Tell 'em you were talking through your hat."

Gregg obeyed. In a moment he was talking once more with the director of the F.B.I. He spoke for only a short while, and then he hung up, lifting a battered face to Fenn.

"It's too late," he said. "Those three men have just left. They took the train for Hill City. They'll arrive at 7:40 tonight."

"Three men?" Fenn asked, puzzled.

"Yes. They're coming unofficially."

"Ah, so!" said Fenn, his eyes glittering under the thick brows. "And their names?"

"Kerrigan, Murdoch and Klaw."

Fenn repeated the names thoughtfully. "Kerrigan and Murdoch and Klaw, eh? Well, we'll handle them. They shouldn't be any trouble at all. As for you, Gregg, go home and stay there till your face gets better. And watch your step!"

"My daughter—"

"Your daughter stays in jail. We'll cook up a couple more charges to hold her on. And in case we should become dissatisfied with the way you work for us, why—" to emphasize what he meant, he smashed his right fist into the palm of his left hand— "*whack!*" He winked. "Get the idea, Gregg?"

He turned and motioned to the gunman at the door. "You stay with *Mister* Gregg, Patsy. Go home with him. You'll be a sort of—er—bodyguard for him, in case he gets any notions. I'll send someone to relieve you at night."

Patsy grinned. "A pleasure, Mister Commissioner!" he said.

Rory Fenn went out, followed by the other two thugs.

"Kerrigan, Murdoch and Klaw!" he was saying amusingly as he walked down the hall. "Three guys who think they can work wonders! Well, well! We'll have to give them a little idea of what it's all about!"

CHAPTER 2
OPEN UP—FOR
THE SUICIDE SQUAD!

WHEN THE Washington train arrived at Hill City at 7:40, Stephen Klaw emerged from it alone. As he made his way from the train platform to the vast concourse of the brilliantly lighted Union Station, his hands were dug deep in his coat pockets. He walked with an easy, swinging stride.

Stephen Klaw was so slim and wiry that one might have taken him, at first glance, for a kid just out of college. One good look at his cold, slate-gray eyes, though, would have told anyone that here was no callow youth, but a trained fighting man.

He appeared to be lost in thought as he made his way across the station toward the row of telephone booths. Yet he did not fail to notice the four hard-faced men standing near the information booth in the center of the station. The dominant figure in the group was a huge brute of a chap, with a flat nose and black, vicious eyes under heavy, bushy brows. Two of the others looked like thugs, but there was the flash of shields under their carelessly opened coats The fourth was a small, pinch-faced man with frightened eyes. Klaw knew that one. It was Neddy Teek, who had once done time in Leavenworth for impersonating a Federal officer. Klaw had arrested him. He guessed that Teek was here for the sole purpose of identifying him.

On the way to the phone booths, Klaw allowed his glance to swing around the entire area of the spacious concourse. He spotted a big, blond, narrow-waisted man with the shoulders of a stevedore, sitting on a bench and reading a newspaper. Another man, dark and handsome, with the lithe grace of a jungle beast, was standing at the magazine stand, talking with the sales girl.

Both those men gave Stephen Klaw a quick, almost imperceptible nod. Klaw went on as if he had not seen them, and entered one of the phone booths in the row against the east wall.

He inserted a nickel in the phone, and dialed a number. Watching out of the corner of his eye, he saw the four men at the information desk walking over toward the booth. The little, pinch-faced informer turned and made for the street exit, as if he wanted no part of what was to follow. The big fellow with the flat nose hurried over and stepped into the booth next to Klaw's, while the other two loitered just outside, their right hands fidgeting up near their neckties.

Stephen Klaw smiled. He waited till he got his connection, and then spoke in a very loud voice, so that the man in the next booth would have no trouble hearing.

"Hello. Is this District Attorney Gregg?"

A thin, faltering voice came back to him over the wire: "Yes. This is Gregg."

"This is Stephen Klaw. I've just arrived at Union Station, and I'm contacting you according to instructions. Where can I meet you?"

There was a moment's silence. Then Gregg said, "I'm very sorry, Mr. Klaw, but the situation has changed since I spoke to

your director. There is really nothing you can do here in Hill City.
I—I'm afraid I was laboring under a misapprehension. Mayor
Bledd has done nothing illegal. Please forget the whole matter."

KLAW'S EYES narrowed. He lowered his voice. "Did they
get to you, Mr. Gregg? Did they put the screws on you?"

"Y-yes."

"Can you talk freely now?"

"No."

"Is someone there with you?"

"Yes."

"How many?"

"Only one."

"Can you answer my questions?"

"Well—yes."

"All right. Do you still want to go on with this thing?"

"Yes!"

"Have they got something on you?"

"Well, not exactly."

"All right," said Steve. "Don't go away. I'll be over to talk to
you."

"No, no!" Gregg exclaimed. "You mustn't. You must leave Hill
City by the next train, and go back to Washington. You must
drop the whole thing—"

"Sure," said Stephen Klaw, raising his voice once more. "I'll
drop it after I've cleaned it up! Good-by, Mr. Gregg."

He hung up, pushed open the door of the booth, and stepped
out.

At the same time, the flat-nosed man came out of the next

booth. He signaled to the two thugs, and they moved in swiftly, arranging themselves on either side of Klaw. The one on the left grinned and pulled back his coat, showing a badge. In his right hand he held a gun.

"This is an arrest, mister," he said.

Steve smiled pleasantly. "How nice! What's the charge?"

Fenn pushed around in front of him. "You'll hear the charge soon enough, *Mister* Klaw!" he said. "Come on!"

He turned and led the way, not to the street, but toward the south end of the building, where the executive offices of the railroad station were located. The two thugs seized Klaw's arms, and propelled him after Fenn.

Steve allowed himself to be led across the station. Several people turned to stare at the group, eyeing the naked guns in the hands of the two thugs. But no one dared to interfere or to ask questions, for the city had already been given a taste of the brutality of Mayor Bledd.

Rory Fenn led the way up a flight of stairs, and pushed open the door marked, "Public Relations Manager."

He grinned and said, "I got the railroad to lend me an office for this little interview. I'm sure you'll like it, *Mister* Klaw."

He waited until the two gunmen had brought Klaw inside, then he closed and locked the door.

"If this is an arrest," Steve suggested mildly, "you ought to take me to a station house."

Fenn looked him over thoughtfully. "When we get through with you, Mister Klaw," he said, "you won't care where you're taken." He motioned to the two thugs. "Grab him!"

Each of them seized one of Klaw's arms, holding him tight.

Fenn, grinning wickedly, raised his right fist, bunched in a hard knot. He smashed a blow at Steve's face.

Stephen Klaw's body did not move in the grip of the two gunmen. But his head jerked an inch or two to the right, and Fenn's huge fist whistled harmlessly past his ear. At the same time, Klaw's left foot kicked out in a lightning movement, catching Fenn square in the shin.

The big bruiser uttered a yell of pain and began to dance around. The two gorillas held on to Steve.

Rory Fenn burst into a string of profanity and came lunging at Steve, with his big fist swinging viciously.

Someone began to pound on the door, and Fenn's fist stopped in midair.

"Who is it?" he growled.

"It's me—Neddy Teek!" the informer's whining voice came from the corridor. "Lemme in, quick, Rory!"

Fenn scowled and went to the door. He unlocked it and yanked it open. "What the hell do you want?"

The stumbling figure of Neddy Teek came hurtling into the room, propelled by a violent shove from behind.

And then, following Neddy, two men came into the room like thunderbolts, shoulder to shoulder, with guns in their hands and cold, set smiles on their lips. They were the big, blond man and the dark, handsome man who had exchanged nods with Klaw out in the station concourse. They were Johnny Kerrigan and Dan Murdoch—the other two-thirds of the Suicide Squad.

IN ONE swift glance, Kerrigan and Murdoch sized up the

situation in the room. They did not have to exchange a single word with Klaw. These three men had worked together so long that they operated like clockwork. They constituted the smoothest-running fighting machine that had ever come to grips with the overlords of crime. And their team-work was half the reason.

For instance, when they had left Washington that day, Klaw had taken the train, while Kerrigan and Murdoch had hopped the late plane, arriving an hour earlier. And Klaw had known, with supreme confidence, that his two sidekicks would be in the Union Station waiting for him, ready to back up any play he might make.

All three of them should have been dead long ago. It was a legend in the underworld that they went out seeking death deliberately—but that the Grim Reaper always appeared to be ducking them.

Unofficially, they were known as the Suicide Squad, the Three Black Sheep of the F.B.I. Johnny Kerrigan had once punched a Senator's son in the nose. Dan Murdoch had shot a croupier to death in a crooked gambling house, when the croupier thought he had the drop on Murdoch. And Stephen Klaw had once told a Congressional Investigating Committee to go to hell when it tried to reprimand him for shooting to kill in a fight with gangsters.

Any other three men guilty of such high misdemeanors would have been summarily dismissed from the service. But the personal reputations and accomplishments of Kerrigan and Murdoch and Klaw were such that public opinion would have been aroused to fury if they had been discharged. So the director of the F.B.I. had seized upon the excuse to retain them in the service. But as a sop to the powers that be, he had promised that they would not be assigned to any routine jobs in which they might give offense to people in high places. He had agreed that they would be used only for undertakings so dangerous that volunteers had to be asked for.

And that was the way Kerrigan and Murdoch and Klaw wanted it. No routine bank embezzlements or investment trust frauds for then. They lived dangerously, and they lived fast, and for them tomorrow was a day which might never come.

As they stood now in this room, Rory Fenn and those others must have felt something of the dynamic fearlessness and the challenge to life which these three breathed. Certainly the cringing Neddy Teek felt it.

He had fallen to the floor at Rory Fenn's feet, and he was whining, "I couldn't help it, Rory. I hadda trick you to open the door. These two guys are Kerrigan and Murdoch. I never saw them in the station, because I was watching the train gate. They grabbed me just now, and made me call out to you. If I hadn't done it, they'd have killed me."

Rory Fenn ripped out an oath, and went for his gun. At the same time, the two gorillas who were holding Steve Klaw let go of him and swung their own weapons to shoot at Kerrigan and Murdoch.

Dan Murdoch, with that grim smile still upon his dark and handsome face, fired once. The big gun jumped in his hand, and the hoodlum on Stephen Klaw's right was hurled backward as if he had been struck by a ten-ton sledgehammer. Simultaneously, an automatic appeared in Klaw's right hand, and somehow its muzzle was up and belching flame at the second thug. The shot caught the man in the left shoulder and spun him around like a weather-vane, with his arms outstretched. He went sliding across the floor and ended up against a desk, huddled on the carpet, and moaning. Klaw's gun and Murdoch's had barked almost in unison.

A split-second later, Johnny Kerrigan reached Rory Fenn in a flying leap. Fenn had his gun out of its holster. Johnny smashed down with his revolver, struck Fenn's wrist. The big bruiser let go of the gun, uttering a cry of pain. He stood disarmed, staring vindictively at Kerrigan.

Johnny chuckled, kicked the fallen gun over toward a corner. Then he looked at Klaw and said, "Hello, Shrimp. Looks like these lads aren't so tough after all."

CHAPTER 3
DEAD OR ALIVE

DAN MURDOCH was blowing smoke out of his gun barrel. "What happened before we got here, Shrimp?" he asked.

"Nothing much," said Steve. "Just that this nice man was telling me a few things. The interview was beginning to get interesting when you mopes barged in."

He looked over at Fenn. "You can go on with that lecture you were giving me," he said amiably.

Rory Fenn glared at him. "You and your two pals are cooked," he rasped. He glanced over at his two gunmen, who were groaning on the floor and trying to stop the flow of blood from their wounds. "You can't get out of this station. I got police all around. There'll be a charge of assault with intent to kill. You three birds will go in the can—where we have ways of breaking tough guys!"

A crowd of people were running toward the room from all directions in the station, and among them were half a dozen uniformed patrolmen, as well as a couple of plainclothes men with riot guns.

Johnny Kerrigan closed the door in the faces of the mob and locked it. Then he turned around, grinning.

"Let's hear all about this jail of yours, mister," he said, and advanced ominously upon Fenn, putting his gun away. There was a hard glint in his eye.

Rory Fenn backed up. "Hey! What're you gonna do?"

"Why, as long as you're going to be so tough with us in your jail," Johnny said silkily, "I figure we might as well take it out on you in advance."

He feinted with his left; and Fenn blocked awkwardly. Johnny stepped in and smashed a right to Fenn's heart. It staggered him. The man was big, but he wasn't in condition. He began to gasp for breath from that single blow. All the weight of those powerful stevedore shoulders of Kerrigan's had been behind the punch.

Johnny stepped in after him, his big fists hammering like riveting machines—*one, two—one, two—one, two.* He bore the burly Rory Fenn backward until he ended up against the wall, trying ineffectually to cover himself. Johnny landed a sweet one on the button, and Fenn folded forward and sank to the floor, his eyes rolling.

Johnny massaged his knuckles, turned his back on the motionless figure of Fenn. He grinned.

Stephen Klaw nodded. "Very nice work, mope. Only I would have enjoyed the privilege myself. Now—let's see about getting out of here."

The clamor outside the locked door had become terrific. Someone was shouting, "Open up! Open up or we'll shoot the lock out!"

ONE OF the two wounded thugs was groaning, writhing on the floor in pain. The other had fainted. Rory Fenn did not move. But the pinch-faced Neddy Teek scrambled to his feet.

Dan Murdoch, who was nearest Teek, grabbed him by the scruff of his neck, and lifted him off the floor.

"Where do you think *you're* going?"

"Lemme go with you!" Neddy Teek gasped. "Rory Fenn will never forgive me for tricking him into opening the door. When he comes to, he—he'll beat my skull in!"

Murdoch let him down to the floor. "So you want to come with us?" He laughed harshly, and jerked his head toward the door, where they could hear the mob yelling.

"Hear that? When we go out of here, we go out shooting. You still want to come along?"

A sly look came into Teek's face. "You don't have to go out that way," he said.

Kerrigan, Murdoch and Klaw looked quickly at one another.

Neddy pointed to a closet door in the left wall of the office.

"That ain't no closet. Rory looked over the layout here before figuring the play. He figured if the three of you came off the train together, he'd want some back way to get extra men in here, if necessary. That's why he picked this room. That door leads into a storeroom. There's another door there that takes you out to the Dispatcher's Room."

"Well!" said Murdoch. "In that case, what are we waiting for?"

A voice outside was bellowing. "Okay, turn that riot gun on the lock. Everybody stand back. Look out for ricochets!"

"Listen," said Johnny Kerrigan rebelliously. "Should we run away from a gang of yellow-bellies like those out there? I vote we go out the front way."

"Well," Murdoch said, with a speculative gleam in his eye, "you've got something there, Johnny. I believe we could account for a nice batch of those birds before they got us all—"

"No, no!" yelled Neddy Teek. "For God's sake, don't be fools. What's the use of getting yourselves killed? It'll leave me up in the air. Come on out the side way!"

Murdoch's eyes had an anticipatory look in them, which the others knew only too well. It was the familiar gleam that came when he began to smell a good fight. "What do you say, Shrimp?" he asked Klaw.

Neddy Teek whirled around to Steve. "Don't let them go out there, Mr. Klaw. For Gawd's sake, don't. How can you help anybody in this town if you're all dead?"

"I think he's right, mopes," Klaw said to Kerrigan and Murdoch. "We owe it to Gregg, and the others in Hill City who need help, to stay alive. We go out the back way."

Johnny Kerrigan sighed regretfully.

"Okay, then. The back way it is."

An authoritative voice outside was calling, "You in there! We got a riot gun trained on the lock. We give you one minute to come out with your hands in the air—if you don't, we come in with guns blasting!"

Murdoch led Neddy Teek out through the storeroom door, going none too willingly. Klaw waited for Johnny, to make sure he didn't yield to one of his sudden, rash impulses. But Johnny was thinking of something else which had just occurred to him.

"Wait a second," he said.

He was stooping over the unconscious body of Rory Fenn, and going through the man's pockets. He came up with a bunch of keys.

"These may come in handy," he grinned. "Maybe one of them is the key to the jail. And who knows—we may yet need to get out of a jail in this town!"

THE FIRST burst of gunfire thundered outside, smashing into the lock, as Kerrigan and Murdoch and Klaw, with Neddy Teek in tow, passed into the storeroom. They threaded their way, in darkness, among piles of baled circulars, to a door at the other side.

Kerrigan went first, with drawn gun. But apparently the crowd hadn't thought of blocking this back way. The Dispatcer's Room was quiet.

The group of scared clerks offered no opposition, and the four men hurried through into the great, vaulted sheds behind the station. Inside, the sound of gunfire had ceased, but now there was a concentrated blowing of police whistles and a wailing of sirens.

Murdoch half carried, half dragged, Neddy Teek through the train sheds and out into a back street. It was dark here, and deserted, except for a couple of trucks that were backed up to the loading platforms. But around the corner there was noise and commotion, and it was drawing closer.

"Well, mopes," Stephen Klaw said grimly, "it looks like the fun is about to begin."

"We could hop a freight train," Neddy Teek offered, "and scram outta town."

He stopped. They were paying no attention to him. Standing there in the dark street, with the hue and cry rising all about them, those three men were coolly laying their plan of campaign.

"We've got to get a headquarters," Klaw was saying. "Some place where we can hide Neddy Teek here, in safety—and a place from which we can operate. If they've got Gregg stymied, we can't depend on him."

"We better find a place in a hurry," said Murdoch. "Here comes a squad car around the corner."

"Okay, mopes," Klaw decided. "There's no better place for us than the station. Back we go."

"Not a bad idea," said Johnny Kerrigan.

He seized Teek by the shoulder, pushed him along in the shadow of the station to an unused loading platform. Stephen Klaw led the way inside. Murdoch brought up the rear, facing backward with drawn gun, in case the occupants of the approaching police car should spot them. Just as Murdoch backed into the protection of the huge sliding door of the loading platform, the clerks from the dispatcher's office, together with the police from inside, came tearing out onto the street. They sighted the squad car.

"Those guys came out this way!" someone shouted.

"Okay," yelled a cop from the police car. "They must have gone down toward the river. We'll get 'em easy!"

The car shot away, with two additional policemen on the running boards. Guns were in their hands.

Murdoch grinned in the darkness. "This station," he said over his shoulder, to Klaw and Kerrigan, "is the last place in the world they'll think of looking for us!"

THE FOUR men felt their way through the dark and empty shed, to a small door at the far side. It opened onto a runway. On the other side of the runway was a luggage desk, and alongside the baggage desk was a door marked "Night Traffic Superintendent."

Stephen Klaw peered out, and saw there was no one in the runway. The baggage clerk must have left his post to see what the shooting was about.

"Wait here," Steve told the others. "I'll go in the Super's office and see if I can locate a blueprint of the station. There must be at least one nice quiet spot where we can leave Teek."

Neddy Teek was shivering with terror. "I tell you, there's no place in the whole town to hide. Hugo Bledd will find us. And if Rory Fenn ever gets his hands on me—"

"Stow it!" Kerrigan said grimly. Then, to Steve, "Go ahead, Shrimp!"

Klaw slipped out and darted across the runway. He turned the knob of the traffic superintendent's door and pushed it open. He stepped into the office.

There was no one inside but a girl. She was red-headed, slim and pretty. She was seated at a typewriter desk, facing the door. On one end of the desk stood a small portable radio receiving set. It was tuned into the short-wave band on police calls, and a raucous voice was coming out of the receiver. It was apparently one of the cops in the radio car, talking on a two-way circuit. He was saying:

"Men escaped toward river. Car 14 in pursuit. Send more cars into river-front territory to help bottle them up!"

Another voice, apparently speaking from police headquarters, acknowledged the report, then barked:

"Orders! All cars converge on riverfront section. Block all streets from Twenty-third north to Fortieth along the river. Let no one through without proper identification. If necessary, search every house where these three men might be taking refuge. They are dangerous and desperate. Shoot to kill! These are my personal orders. Any police officer who kills or captures one, or all of these men will receive a bonus of a year's pay, plus immediate promotion to a captaincy. Remember, I want them dead or alive! I repeat: All cars converge...."

Stephen Klaw heard that much over the radio as he came into the office. Then the red-headed girl stood up behind her desk. With her left hand she shut off the radio, breaking the speaker's voice in the middle of a word. With her right hand she picked up an automatic pistol from alongside the typewriter, and slipped off the safety catch. She pointed it at Klaw. Her eyes were flashing.

"Stand still and raise your hands to the air," she ordered, "or I'll shoot you to death!"

CHAPTER 4
BLUECOATS FOR G-MEN

STEPHEN KLAW gave the girl a bleak grin. He had his right hand in his coat pocket. He did not take it out, and he did not raise his hands above his head.

Instead, he came slowly toward the desk. "Go ahead and shoot, sister," he said softly. Her eyes never left him. She was standing stiffly, one hand at her breast, the other gripping the pistol tightly, pointing it straight at his heart. Her fingers curled around the trigger. She was biting her lower lip.

Stephen Klaw came up within three feet of the desk. He faced her directly across it. "Well," he asked, "why don't you shoot?" She kept the gun steady. He noticed that her hand did not shake. But she was breathing fast.

"You—you don't look like a thug," she said doubtfully.

"Thank you." He smiled. "Are you afraid of thugs—here in the heart of the railroad station?"

"I'm not afraid of anyone!" she flashed. "I—I can take care of myself—with this gun. None of Hugo Bledd's murderous thugs will get in here."

"I'm glad to hear you say that," Steve told her. "I'm not one of Bledd's thugs. I'm one of the men they're hunting."

There was a look of doubt in her eyes. But there was also an expression that seemed to indicate she would like to believe him.

"Can you prove that?" she asked.

He shrugged. "Suppose if I were one of Bledd's gunmen, I would have shot you by this time."

Her lip curled. "With what?"

"With this!" He took his hand out of the right-hand coat pocket. It was gripping a black .25 caliber gunmetal automatic.

Her eyes widened. For a moment she was off guard.

Steve reached over in a lightning motion with his left hand and gripped the butt of her pistol, curling his fingers around the trigger guard and turning the muzzle away from his heart. She began to struggle, saw it was useless. She let go of the gun, and slumped.

"Well," she said, "you fooled me. For a minute I thought you were an honest man. Well—what are you going to do to me?"

"Nothing," said Stephen Klaw. He put his own gun away, and laid her pistol on the desk.

"Pick it up!" he ordered.

She stared at him, unable to comprehend.

"Pick it up!" he repeated.

Sourly, she obeyed.

"Go ahead," he said. "You can shoot me now if you want to."

Her lower lip began to tremble. "I—I don't understand."

"I'm Stephen Klaw," he told her harshly. "Special agent of the Federal Bureau of Investigation. My two partners, Johnny

Kerrigan and Dan Murdoch, are outside. We're being hunted all over town by Mayor Bledd's men. If you've been putting on an act for me, claiming you're an enemy of Bledd's, now's your chance to earn a big reward, by shooting me. But I think I've sized you up right, and I'm taking a chance on you."

"Oh!" was all she said. A bit of moisture appeared in her eyes. She slumped back into her chair, put the pistol down, and began to cry.

"Cut it!" said Steve. "This is no time for hysterics. What are you crying about?"

She raised her eyes to his. Bravely, she wiped the tears away. "You don't understand. I—I've been waiting for five days—waiting for them to come and kill me. I—I thought you were their executioner!"

"What are you talking about?" Steve demanded.

"I'm Elsie Hope. My father, John Hope, was night traffic superintendent. He—he was also a city councilman. When Hugo Bledd became mayor, my father was one of the councilmen who were killed. They—they beat him to death! I saw it from the window of our home. I—I recognized the men who did it. But when I went to the police station, they told me I'd better forget about it if I wanted to stay alive. I tried Judge Rotherwell, too, but he wouldn't listen to me. Ever since father's death, I've been coming down here to the office. I know the work, because I acted as father's secretary. I'm keeping things running till the railroad appoints another night traffic superintendent."

"I see," Steve said softly.

SHE ROSE impulsively. "I'm sure they intend to kill me. They know I'll try every means possible to avenge father. And they know, if there's ever a real investigation, I'll be able to identify his killers. That's why I've been waiting every day, with a loaded gun."

Steve came around the desk and put a hand on her shoulder.

"Keep your chin up, Elsie," he said. "My partners and I are here to clean up this town. We'll pay off for your dad."

Her eyes were shining. "I'll do anything to help you!"

"All right. What I want is a blueprint of the layout of this station. There must be some spot in here that we can use for headquarters."

"You don't need a blueprint!" she exclaimed. "I know just the place. There's a private car sidetracked in the shed. It used to belong to Nick Torlona, the gangster Hugo Bledd worked for. When Torlona went to jail, the rent was never paid to the railroad, and we had to seize it. It's never been used since. It's equipped with a generator for independent light, and it has a radio and an electric kitchen...."

Steve seized her hand. "Enough said. It's made to order. Come on!"

He barely gave her a chance to get her hat and coat and purse, and fairly thrust her out of the office.

They got out onto the runway, and stopped short. Kerrigan was standing in the open, with a gun in each hand, covering two uniformed policemen—one a patrolman and the other a sergeant. Both cops had their hands in the air and looked shame-faced and uncomfortable. Behind Kerrigan, Steve Klaw could see Murdoch and Neddy Teek peering out from the interior of the loading room.

Steve chuckled. "Bag something, mope?"

Johnny Kerrigan grinned. "These two gents have a radio car outside. They got the notion they ought to look in here for us. They made the mistake of not seeing us first."

"Well," said Steve, "I guess we'll have to take them along. Follow us, mopes. We're going to live on the fat of the land— with the help of Elsie, here."

Ten minutes later, they were installed in a luxurious private car named "HONEY."

It was a long and spacious car, with four private bedrooms, a lounging room, a kitchenette, toilet and bath and an observation platform.

"Not bad," Johnny Kerrigan said admiringly. "But what happens if someone spots the lights in here?"

"Nothing happens," Elsie Hope said with a smile. "There are half a dozen private cars in this shed, and very often the owners occupy them the night before starting on a trip. When their time of departure arrives, the brakemen get the traveling orders and simply couple them onto the train, without even waking up the occupants. So until a traveling order comes through, no one will disturb us."

Neddy Teek was prowling around nervously, peering out past the edges of the drawn blinds, and sweating profusely.

"I'll never feel safe," he muttered, "till I'm about a million miles from Rory Fenn."

They had tied up their two policeman prisoners, and put them in one of the private bedrooms. Now Kerrigan and Murdoch and Klaw got in a huddle and whispered for five minutes. When they came out of the huddle they were grinning.

"We're leaving you for a while, Elsie," Steve announced. "Put out the lights and sit tight. We'll be back soon. But first, we have to make a little quick change."

KLAW AND Kerrigan went into the bedroom with the two prisoners. In a few minutes they came out, and Murdoch started to laugh. Elsie Hope and Neddy Teek just stared. Steve and Johnny were wearing the captured men's uniforms. Johnny made a very handsome looking sergeant, but Steve Klaw's uniform was just a bit too large for him.

Neddy Teek groaned. "My Gawd! Are you guys going into town?"

"Uh-huh!" said Johnny. "Okay, Dan, grab him."

Dan Murdoch, who was standing nearest to Neddy, seized his arms, and lifted him off the floor.

"Hey!" yelled Teek. "What you gonna do?"

"Sorry, Neddy," Stephen Klaw told him. "But we have to make sure we can trust you. The three of us are leaving for a while, and we don't want you getting any ideas."

They fixed up a nice gag for him, and tied his hands and feet with towels, and put him in another, larger bedroom. "I guess you'll be safe for a while," Steve said to Elsie.

She showed him her gun.

Steve nodded. "You'd make a nice addition to the F.B.I., kid!" The three of them climbed out of the private car, and Elsie locked the door.

"Okay, mopes," said Steve.

They made their way through the shed and out to the runway. There were people here now, and the baggage clerk had come back on the job. A police detective was standing at the door of the night traffic superintendent's office.

He saw the three of them, and waved his hand. "Come here, will you?"

They went over, Dan Murdoch in the middle, and Klaw and Kerrigan on either side. The detective scowled.

"You guys know where the girl is that works in this office?"

"Ain't she in there?" Johnny asked.

"Naw. I got a warrant for her. Were you inside the station just now?"

"Yeah," said Johnny. "But we didn't see her."

"Who's this?" the detective asked, jerking his thumb at Dan.

"Aw, just a bum we picked up."

"Listen," said the detective. "I never seen you two guys before."

"So what?" said Johnny. "We never seen you before, either. Come to think of it, maybe you're one of those three guys that's on the lam."

The detective grunted. "You're crazy. Here's my shield!"

He flashed the badge in the palm of his hand. It was gold, and it said, "Lieutenant."

"There's lots of new guys on the force these days." He grinned.

"Hmm," said Johnny Kerrigan. He turned and looked at Murdoch. "Like it, Dan?"

Dan nodded. "It'll do. I always wanted to be a lieutenant."

"Right," said Johnny. He stepped up and took the lieutenant by the arm. "Come with us, please."

"Hey! Are you nuts?"

Stephen Klaw stepped up and took his other arm in a grip of iron. "Naughty, naughty," he said. "You mustn't call my partner nuts."

"What the hell is this?" demanded the detective.

HE TRIED to yank himself free, but couldn't budge their grip. Between them, Steve and Johnny hustled him down the runway, with Dan trailing along.

There were several people on the platform now. They stared.

The struggling lieutenant yelled, "Help! Help me, someone! These guys are kidnaping me! I'm Lieutenant Lemson! Them guys are impostors!"

But behind them, Dan was smiling, and motioning to the passers-by.

"Drunk!" he said to one of them.

They took their man through the shed and back to the "HONEY."

"Open up, Elsie!" Murdoch called.

In a moment they had Lieutenant Lemson inside, and proceeded to treat him like the other prisoners, while Elsie watched. Dan took his badge, gun, handcuffs and identification papers, and stowed them in his own pockets.

"It looks like they weren't going to kill you right off, Elsie," Steve told her. "They were arresting you first. Here's the warrant."

It was signed by Judge Rotherwell, and it specified no criminal charge, but ordered her arrest as a material witness in the investigation of her father's death.

Elsie's face was white. "It's the same as killing me. Terrible things happen to people in the Hill City jail, now that Bledd's toughs are in charge. Men and women are tortured and beaten. The police make arrests on the flimsiest charges. Only today they arrested the daughter of District Attorney Norton Gregg, on a complaint of reckless driving. I—I'm wondering what's happening to poor Susan."

Steve gripped her shoulder. "You're sure Susan Gregg was arrested today?"

"Yes. Susan and I went to school together. I called the house this morning, and Mrs. Gregg told me."

Steve gave Dan and Johnny a significant look. "That explains about Gregg!"

They left without further explanation.

Once more they made their way out of the shed, and this time they went into the street behind the loading platform. There, at the curb, was the radio car they had captured.

Johnny Kerrigan took the wheel.

"First stop, Hill City *Daily News*, Johnny!" said Steve.

Dan grinned as they pulled away. "And don't forget, you punks, to give me the respect due to a lieutenant of police."

Johnny's answer was a loud and eloquent raspberry.

CHAPTER 5
"REMAIN AT EASE!"

THE STREETS were full of police. The hue and cry for the Suicide Squad was in full swing.

Johnny turned on the radio, and they caught the police orders, which were issuing from headquarters with staccato speed:

"Confidential to all police cars. It is Mayor Bledd's personal wish that the three men known as Kerrigan and Murdoch and Klaw be captured or killed before midnight. There is a rumor going around town that these men are agents of the Federal Bureau of Investigation. This is untrue. These men are criminals, posing as Federal Agents. No police officer need feel any fear about shooting to kill. Mayor Bledd promises full protection to any officer who does so. Treat these men like mad dogs...."

"That's us," said Johnny. "Now we're mad dogs. Wow! Let's go up and take a bite out of Hugo Bledd's pants!"

"Not yet," Steve said grimly.

"Well, we better do it quick," said Johnny, "before they get the dog catchers after us. What about phoning the Chief in Washington?"

"Nix," said Steve. "How would we sound, telling him we just got here and they've got us on the run already?" He was interrupted by the police announcer over the radio once more:

"Car 41, why don't you report? Car 41, where are you? Why don't you report? Car 41, call in at once. Standing by...."

Murdoch frowned. "Car 41. Could that be us?"

Steve opened the window at his side and leaned out and looked at the number painted on the door.

"It's us all right," he said. "Precinct 18, Car 41. I guess we ought to report in."

He flipped over the switch of the two way radio, and spoke into the transmitter: "Car 41 reporting. What the hell do you want?"

"Sergeant Gumber!" exclaimed the voice of the police announcer. "What the hell do you mean by talking like that? Where are you?"

"This ain't Sergeant Gumber," Steve said. "Gumber is driving. This is Patrolman Nuggin."

He was using the name of the man whose clothes he had usurped.

"What's the matter with you, Nuggin?" the announcer asked. "Why is Gumber driving?"

"I hurt my arm."

"All right, all right, why didn't you call back before? Did you meet Lieutenant Lemson at the Union Station? Did you arrest that girl yet?"

"Yeah," said Steve. "We got her."

"Okay, you and Gumber know your orders. You know what to do with her."

"Sure. We'll bring her in."

"No, no, you fool."

"You mean you want her knocked off?"

"Listen, Nuggin," said the announcer. "If you're gonna start

148

being a wise-guy, it ain't going to be healthy for you around this town. You know what you were told to do. Let her try to escape, and then put a bullet in her back. Do it in a busy part of town, where people will see she was trying to get away. Just give her a chance, and she'll grab it. She's a spitfire. Did you have any trouble?"

"No," said Steve, his blood boiling.

"All right, then," the announcer hurried on. "Get through with it, and rush over to the riverfront. We need every car to round up those three mugs."

"Okay," said Steve.

He shut off the radio, and threw a side glance at Johnny and Dan.

"Boy," said Johnny, "if I had known what that Lieutenant Lemson and those two guys were up to, I'd have—!"

HE WAS guiding the car through the busiest section of the city, and it was readily apparent that the town was in a turmoil. People were congregated at corners, talking and gesticulating.

But the excitement over the river-front manhunt did not interfere with the nightly pleasure-pursuits of the city. The streets were well-filled with throngs on their way to the theatre or to the many gambling and vice dens which had sprung up within the few days of Mayor Bledd's administration.

Johnny swung into a side street and pulled up at the curb in front of the rambling building of the Hill City *Daily News*. The building was a beehive.

There was a crowd in the street here, too, all craning their necks to see the bulletins which were being posted outside the first floor windows. These bulletins were printed in big, foot-high letters, and two floodlights streamed down upon them so that it was easy to read the news. One bulletin said:

BOGUS G-MEN TRAPPED IN RIVER FRONT DISTRICT! SWIFT CAPTURE EXPECTED. CITY COUNCIL VOTES MAYOR BLEDD UNLIMITED POWER TO DEAL WITH DISORDER AND CRIME

The one next to it read:

DISTRICT ATTORNEY GREGG PRAISES MAYOR BLEDD FOR EFFORTS TO SECURE ORDER. GREGG STATES THAT ALL TROUBLE IS BEING FOMENTED BY POLITICAL ENEMIES OF MAYOR BLEDD.

A man was out on the platform up there, tacking up a third notice:

F.B.I. CHIEF DENIES SENDING G-MEN! DIRECTOR SAYS THREE MEN WHO ATTACKED COMMISSIONER RORY FENN AND SHOT TWO DETECTIVES IN UNION STATION ARE NOT SPECIAL AGENTS. THEY ARE BELIEVED TO BE GUNMEN BROUGHT IN FROM OTHER CITIES TO DISCREDIT MAYOR BLEDD'S ADMINISTRATION.

Stephen Klaw got out of the police car, straightening his ill-fitting uniform. Dan Murdoch and Johnny Kerrigan followed.

Steve gestured up toward the bulletins. "Nice propaganda," he said bitterly. "They'll have us eating babies next."

The three of them pushed their way through to the doorway.

A uniformed policeman was standing on guard at the entrance. He touched his cap, at sight of the sergeant's stripes on Johnny's uniform, and let them through.

They went up in the elevator to the second floor, and walked through the hall, being elbowed about by hurrying copy boys and reporters. They entered the news room, and Johnny stopped a sweating man in shirt-sleeves.

"Where'll we find the owner?"

The man pushed Johnny out of the way. "Don't bother me!" he growled. "We go to press in fifteen minutes!"

Johnny grabbed his arm. "It'll only take you a fifth of a minute to be polite, mister."

The man stopped short, took a look at his uniform, and gulped. "I—I'm sorry, Sergeant. I thought you were another one of those discharged cops coming in here to belly-ache about being canned off the force without pension. I guess you're one of Mayor Bledd's new men."

"Yeah," said Johnny. "We're new men. Where's the owner's office?"

"There's Mr. Rick's office, over at the back of the news room. He's the managing editor—"

"Not the managing editor," Kerrigan said. "The owner."

"Oh. You mean Watson Blount." The man grinned. "He don't count any more. He's got nothing to say. You better do your business with Mr. Rick."

Kerrigan sighed. "Look," he said patiently. "We don't want advice. We just want to know where to find Watson Blount."

The man shrugged. "Okay, okay. Go out that side door and up one flight of stairs. His office is at the top."

"Thanks," said Johnny, and let the fellow go. Then the three of them went through the news room and up the stairs to Blount's office.

"Okay, Steve," said Johnny. "You take it from here."

STEVE NODDED. He put his hand on the door knob, and pushed the door open without knocking. He stepped inside with Kerrigan and Murdoch.

A gray-haired man was sitting at his desk, with his face in his hands. Over at one side, in a chair, with his feet on the window-sill, was a very hard-faced mug.

"Remain at ease, mister!" Stephen Klaw said pleasantly, producing an automatic.

The mug put his feet down on the floor, opened his mouth in surprise, but did not go for a gun.

Smiling affably, Dan Murdoch went over to him, took the revolver out of his holster, fanned him for other weapons, and then stepped back.

The gray-haired man at the desk had raised his head. He was watching the proceedings dully.

"What do you want from me now?" he asked. "Hasn't Bledd done enough to me already?"

Stephen Klaw came over to the desk. "What do you mean, Mr. Blount?"

"What do I mean?" Blount exploded. "I'll tell you what I

mean! Bledd has taken my newspaper away from me! He's put his own man in as managing editor, and a dozen discredited newspaper men from all over the country are in here now, assisting Rick. They've replaced my old employees. Rick runs the paper—my paper, that I spent forty years building up—and I have to sit here with a thug guarding me, and sign everything that's put in front of me. I have to okay the publication of lying stories about my friends, and I have to sit by while Rick writes editorials praising Bledd's murderous activities. That's what I mean!"

Steve threw a side glance at Kerrigan, who nodded. "Tell him," Johnny said softly.

"Okay!" Steve nodded. "Mr. Blount, you've got your paper back. From now on, it's your paper again."

Watson Blount stared at him, then swiveled his glance to Johnny Kerrigan's uniform. "I—I don't understand. You—you're new men on the force. You must be Bledd's men…."

Steve laughed. "We're new, all right. But we're not exactly working for the mayor. This—" he indicated Johnny—"is Kerrigan, temporarily a sergeant in the Hill City police force. Over there," he waved toward Dan—"is Murdoch, temporarily a lieutenant. And I—" he bowed gravely—"am Klaw, a humble patrolman."

Watson Blount's eyes widened. "Kerrigan, Murdoch and Klaw! The men they're hunting for all over town!"

"Exactly," said Steve. "And we're giving your paper back to you—lock, stock and barrel!"

Blount came out of his chair. "You don't know what you're

talking about, Klaw. You can't do it. You don't realize what you're up against. This man," he motioned toward the mug, who was looking very deflated without his gun, and a little scared at discovering he was in the hands of the Suicide Squad—"this man is only one of a number of armed thugs in charge of the building. They have one of their men at each door, preventing my friends from entering. There are armed hoodlums in the press room, and in the editorial office. I don't dare make a move, because Bledd threatens to destroy the whole building if I don't play ball with him."

"That's fine, Mr. Blount," Steve told him. "We like it tough. Now—are you willing to take a chance with us, or not? Make up your mind quickly. We haven't much time. If you don't want to risk your hide, if you'd rather sit here and watch your paper run by gunmen and murderers, all right, we'll go elsewhere...."

"Wait!" said Watson Blount. His shoulders were suddenly straight, and his head was up. "I'm with you! I don't know what you're going to do, or how you're going to do it. But give me a gun!"

Dan Murdoch grinned, gave him the guard's gun.

"Let's go," said Johnny Kerrigan.

He took the mug by the shoulder and pushed him out the door. "Start something," he begged. "Just start something."

"I ain't starting a thing, Mister Kerrigan," the fellow blubbered.

CHAPTER 6
CITIZENS, ARISE!

THEY WENT down the stairs and along a corridor, avoiding the busy editorial room. Blount led them to the back door of Rick's office.

Steve pushed the door open, took Blount by the arm, and walked in.

Chauncey Rick was at the desk, drinking rye whiskey with three yeggs.

Rick was saying. "Five minutes before press time, and they haven't caught those three guys yet. What the hell, we'll announce their capture anyway." He was writing a headline as he spoke. "I'll say all three were killed resisting arrest. Rory Fenn will never let them get to headquarters alive—"

He stopped, with his mouth open, his pen poised in the air, looking at the group that had come barging in.

"What the hell is the matter now?" he demanded. "Can't you knock?"

Kerrigan, Murdoch and Klaw had guns in their hands.

"Anyone who wants to make something of this," Stephen Klaw said softly, "is welcome to try!"

The three thugs put their drinks down gently. They didn't make any unnecessary or sudden motions.

"What the hell is this?" demanded Rick. "Are you guys nuts?"

One of the thugs said huskily, "Lay off, Rick. These ain't our guys. They—they're the Suicide Squad!"

155

Stephen Klaw's eyes never left Rick. "Get out of that chair," he ordered.

Rick swallowed hard, and tried to bluster. "You can't get away with—"

Stephen Klaw came around the desk and stood alongside his chair. "Do you want it the hard way?" he asked softly.

"Wait!" blurted Rick. He got out of the chair.

Dan Murdoch smiled affably at him and the three gunmen. "Now, if you gentlemen will all line up, with your faces to the wall, I'd be greatly obliged."

They obeyed quickly. Murdoch's courtesy was like the iron hand in the silk glove. He didn't threaten, but they knew he meant business.

Johnny Kerrigan stepped from one to the other, and relieved them of their guns. "In all this artillery that we're gathering," he said pleasantly, "I wouldn't be surprised if we find the cannon that killed Elsie Hope's father."

He watched them keenly, and saw one of the gunmen shift uneasily. He grabbed the man by the shoulder and swung him around. It was the man who had identified them for Rick.

"I seem to know you," said Johnny, who never forgot a face. "Weren't you one of Nick Torlona's hoods in the old days, before he went to Alcatraz? We picked you up once in an automobile racket, but you squeezed out of it. Your name is Gildey, isn't it?"

Gildey avoided Kerrigan's eyes. "I want a lawyer," he said. "You got no right to arrest me. I ain't broke no federal laws."

"You're wrong there," Kerrigan said softly. "We find you here, intimidating a newspaper owner. The Hill City *Daily News* goes through the mail. That makes it interstate commerce, which puts it in our jurisdiction!"

Stephen Klaw pushed Watson Blount into the seat vacated by Chauncey Rick.

"Go to it," he said. "Do your stuff!"

BLOUNT'S EYES were glittering. He snatched up the phone. "Press room!" he snapped. "Break up page one. Hold for new plates!" He listened a moment, then said, "Hold it, Pete!"

He looked up at Stephen Klaw. "Pete, my press foreman, says there's a man with a sawed-off rifle down there, who won't let him take orders from anyone but Rick."

"Ah, so!" said Steve. He looked over at Rick, who was grinning smugly.

"I told you so," said Rick. "You can't pull this and get away with—"

He didn't have to finish, because at a signal from Steve, Dan Murdoch took Rick by the hair and dragged him over to the desk and pushed his face down to the phone.

"Tell that mug with the sawed-off rifle to come right up here!" Dan ordered. "And if you say one word we don't like, I'll chuck you out the window!"

"Damn you," Rick gasped, "let go of me! Gildey, Lobb, Flick! Help—"

Gildey, Lobb and Flick didn't make a move, because Johnny Kerrigan was standing very close to them, with a gun in his hand. He was grinning.

Dan Murdoch sighed. He pulled Rick away from the phone by the hair. "I see you have to be convinced, my friend." He dragged him over to the window and started to push his head through.

"No, no!" Rick screamed. "Don't—"

Murdoch said nothing. He got a grip on the sent of Rick's pants.

"Stop!" gasped Rick. "Stop. I'll—I'll do whatever you say!"

"All right," said Murdoch.

He dragged the man back to the phone. Rick gasped into it, "Put Harris on the phone."

He waited a moment, then said, "Harris, this is Rick. Come right up here. I've got to see you."

Murdoch took him away from the phone. Blount was writing busily. They waited three minutes, and then Harris came into the office through the front door. He was carrying his sawed off rifle under his arm, and scowling.

Just as he stepped into the room, Stephen Klaw, who had been waiting behind the door, stepped out behind him and poked a gun in his ribs.

"You can drop that rifle or not—just as you choose," Steve said indifferently.

Harris stood frozen for an instant, looking at his pals lined up against the wall and at Murdoch and Kerrigan.

"I quit," said Harris. He bent down, and carefully put the rifle on the floor.

Steve pushed him over to the wall to join the others.

WATSON BLOUNT waved the sheet he had completed. "Man!" he exclaimed. "This will explode a bomb under Bledd!"

He scribbled a note to the composing room designating the

use of huge, block-lettered type that would cover the entire front page. The sheet read:

CITIZENS OF HILL CITY, AWAKE! ARISE!
THROW OFF THE DICTATORSHIP
OF GUNMEN AND GANGSTERS!
MASS MEETING TONIGHT AT ELEVEN P.M.
CITY HALL SQUARE, ALL COME.
LEAVE YOUR WOMEN AT HOME!

"Nice stuff," said Steve. "Shoot it."

Blount pressed a button, and a copyboy appeared. "Down to the prep room!" Blount ordered. "Tell Pete to break up page two for the story. Hold the presses till I write it, even if the paper is late!"

When the boy was gone, Blount swung to Steve. "I'll give them the whole story on page two. But I need proof. The only man who has proof is Norton Gregg."

"Go ahead with the story," Steve ordered. "We'll get the proof."

"But wait," Blount protested. "You three can't go away. The minute you leave, these thugs will take over."

Steve was at the bookshelf in the corner, pulling down a fat volume. It was the City Service list of Hill City, giving the name and address of every man on the police force, the fire department and the other city services.

"How many of the old men have been fired off the force by Mayor Bledd?"

"About eight hundred," Blount said.

"Fine," said Steve.

He took the book and went out into the front office. Murdoch came with him. Kerrigan stayed with the thugs.

When Steve appeared, the editorial room became silent at sight of the guns in his and in Murdoch's hands.

"Attention, everybody!" Steve thundered. "Mr. Blount has once more resumed active management of this paper. All those who want to work with him stand up!"

Almost everybody got up.

Steve went from desk to desk, tearing a half dozen pages from the directory at a time, and handing them to each person with a phone at his desk.

"Get on those phones!" he ordered. "Call every cop and fireman in the list. Tell them if they want their old jobs back, and are willing to fight for them, to come right down here and report in Mr. Blount's office."

When he was through distributing the pages, he and Murdoch returned to Blount's office. Already, the clerks, reporters and re-write men were busy.

INSIDE THE office, Johnny Kerrigan had done a nice piece of work. He found that most of the prisoners, having been appointed policemen by Bledd, were equipped with handcuffs. So he used their own handcuffs to link them together in a long chain, with the end men on the line cuffed to the two radiators in the room.

It was less than fifteen minutes before the first of the discharged policemen and firemen began to appear at the News

Building, thirsting for a chance to fight back at the racketeer administration which had deprived them of their livelihood.

Murdoch organized them into squads, placing each squad in a strategic position in the building, and disarming the thugs who were posted there. In a short time the entire plant was in their hands, and the presses were turning swiftly, with Blount's black headlines filling page one, and the story of corruption and murder on page two.

"All right, mopes," said Klaw. "Let's go." The faces of Kerrigan, Murdoch and Klaw were like granite.

They shook hands with Watson Blount, who had a rejuvenated look in his eyes, and went out into the street. The crowd out there had been augmented considerably, for the rumour had spread that big things were doing at the News Building. A group of a hundred and fifty old-timers on the police force was drawn up in military formation, with an ex-captain of police at their head, all dressed in their uniform, with guns belted at their hips.

A lusty cheer rose when they raw Kerrigan and Murdoch and Klaw.

And then they saw a white-haired man with a haggard face pushing through the crowd.

Someone said, "Gregg! That's District Attorney Norton Gregg!"

District Attorney Gregg looked like a man who has endured the tortures of hell. His face was swollen and discolored from the beating he had received at the hands of Rory Fenn, and his white hair was disheveled and matted.

He came straight toward Steve Klaw, and gripped his sleeve.

161

"Good God!" he exclaimed, "You've got to call this off. You can't go on. They've got my daughter, Susan, in jail. They'll beat her to death if you don't stop. Rory Fenn is ready to go to work on her. Bledd himself phoned me—told me to come here! He told me to stop you, or they'll send me Susan's broken body!"

CHAPTER 7
THE BATTLE OF
SUICIDE SQUARE

"LET'S MARCH on the jail!" someone shouted. "We'll take it apart!"

"No, no!" Gregg cried in an agonized voice, "They'd kill Susan!"

Stephen Klaw put a hand on his shoulder. "Gregg," he said gruffly, "have you got the proof to back up your indictments of Bledd and his crowd?"

Gregg's stance met Steve's squarely. "Yes, I have it. But I'm not turning it over while Susan is in their power."

"No," Steve said thoughtfully. "I can't blame you." Suddenly he looked up. "If your daughter were out of there—"

"I'd go the limit!" Gregg exclaimed. "By God, I'd give you enough to put Bledd in jail for a thousand years!"

"All right, then." Steve looked inquiringly at Murdoch and Kerrigan. Both nodded.

As soon as they nodded, Stephen Klaw raised his hands and shouted to the yelling men in the street. "Quiet, everybody! You heard what Gregg told us. Marching on the jail will mean his daughter's death. I ask you all to remain right here. Do nothing until you hear from us. Will you do that?"

There was grumbling among the uniformed men. But in a moment it subsided. The captain at their head said, "We leave everything in your hands. You three men started this, and you can do it your own way—so long as you give us your word you won't quit on us."

"We won't quit!" Steve told them.

He motioned to Gregg to go inside the News Building. The uniformed men remained in the street, with the mob growing denser every minute.

Steve drew the captain aside. "Spread your men out in the Square," he said, "and tell them to keep order, just as if they were on duty. Keep the mob in hand till you hear from us."

The captain nodded acquiescence, and Kerrigan, Murdoch and Klaw climbed into the radio car they had left at the curb.

"To the jail," Stephen Klaw said.

As Johnny drove, Murdoch switched on the short-wave radio. He caught the announcer's voice on the police broadcasting station just finishing an order, and saying, "I will repeat...."

The man went on, "All cars give up hunt for Kerrigan, Murdoch and Klaw. They are in the News Building, and have control of the paper. All cars and all police appointed by Mayor Bledd are ordered to report at once to the City Jail. It is possible that an attack will be made on the jail. Report at once!"

Grimly, silently, the three men sat in the car as it sped across town to the City Jail. When they were within half a dozen blocks

163

of it, they saw straggling men hurrying in the same direction on foot.

"It looks like Bledd is going to hold the jail," Steve said. "We could have got there with those old-timers in time to capture it."

"Yeah," said Johnny. "But what about Susan Gregg?"

"Well," said Steve, "we'll have to go in and get Susan ourselves."

THEY LEFT the car a block from the jail, and walked. At the main entrance, a crowd of men was going in, but each one who entered had to pass inspection. In the courtyard, two sub-machine guns were trained on the entrance, and half a dozen men with riot guns were on watch.

Johnny Kerrigan looked glum. "What do we do?" he asked. "Go right through?"

"Not a chance," said Murdoch. "The idea right now is not to get ourselves killed, but to get inside."

"What about those keys you took from Rory Fenn?" Steve asked of Kerrigan.

Johnny pulled them out. There was a thoughtful look in his eyes. "You think maybe it'll work?"

Steve shrugged. "We can try."

The three of them faded around the corner, and walked down the side street, close to the jail wall. The prison building was an old structure, massive and weather-beaten, occupying a square block, with the County Court House directly behind it. Like many of the old jails of the period in which it had been built, it had a main entrance at the front, and a side entrance on each of the side streets. At the rear it was connected, by an overhead enclosed bridge, with the County Court House.

Kerrigan wanted to try his keys in the door of the side entrance, but there wasn't a chance, for a man with a sawed-off shotgun stood on guard just inside. They passed by nonchalantly, then hurried down the street and across to the County Court House.

The Court House was closed for business, of course, but the front door was open, and they went right in. No one was around, except a couple of cleaning women who paid no attention to them.

They climbed the stairs to the first floor, and Kerrigan silently indicated the passage leading to the overhead bridge. Halfway along the bridge, there was a steel door.

Klaw and Murdoch took their guns out, while Johnny tried key after key from Fenn's bunch, in the keyhole.

Suddenly he said, "This is it!"

The key turned, and the lock squeaked. Kerrigan pushed the door in, and Murdoch and Klaw slipped past him, with their guns pointing ahead. There was no one in the corridor on the other side of the door.

They could hear a lot of noise, and the sounds of the movements of many men, and voices raised in command. Coming out of the corridor, they found themselves in the jail mezzanine, looking down into the lobby below, which was thronged with the men who had been admitted at the front gate. Weapons were being handed out from racks by Rory Fenn.

"Remember, you mugs," Fenn was saying, "this is different

165

from any racket you've ever been in. You ain't working for any outlaw racketeer now. You've got the law on your side. Your boss is the mayor of this town, and everything you do is legal. You can go out there and shoot the guts out of those suckers, and they can't do a thing to you. The only ones we got to worry about are the Federal guys. And we've got them stopped, because there ain't a Federal offense that can bring them legally into this town. So shoot to kill, an' kill plenty of the suckers!"

Johnny Kerrigan was scowling. He took a quick step forward and lifted his gun. Steve Klaw grabbed his arm.

"Hold it, Johnny."

Kerrigan nodded. "Okay. But I want Mr. Rory Fenn for myself when the time comes."

THE THREE of them made their way along the mezzanine, and turned into the cell block. The prisoners were all quiet tonight.

Kerrigan led the way into the cell block, and he almost ran head-on into a jailer with a gun holstered at his side.

The jailer sprang back when he saw Kerrigan, but relaxed at sight of the uniform. "What you doing up here?" he demanded. "Get downstairs."

"Not yet!" Johnny said softly.

He stepped closer to the man, who jumped back in sudden alarm. But he almost fell into the arms of Dan Murdoch, who had sidled in beside him. Murdoch clipped him behind the ear.

Steve Klaw stooped, took a small Yale key from the man's belt, and went down to the other end of the cell block, where there was a locked electric switch-box. He used the key to open the box, and then pulled over the lever. Immediately, the electrical connection opened the locks on the long double row of cell doors.

Murdoch went down the line, talking in a low voice, telling the prisoners that they were free, and to file quietly out through the overhead bridge.

Among all these prisoners there was not a single genuine criminal. Men and women had been thrust indiscriminately in the cells, without bothering to separate them. Some were wives and daughters of city officials; some were small business men who had refused to pay tribute to Bledd's thugs. Among them was a twelve-year-old boy, the son of Judge Rotherwell, who had appointed Bledd to the mayoralty. That explained the jurist's acquiescence in the reign of terror.

Klaw went among the prisoners as they filed out, asking for Susan Gregg. He was told that she had been taken to the mayor's office half an hour ago.

"All right," said Steve. "We'll get her, too." They aided the prisoners to leave, waiting until the last one had passed across the bridge. "Get over to the News Building," Steve told them. "Tell the cops there to march down to the jail and wait, a block away, till they hear fireworks and then to come in shooting!"

As soon as the last of the prisoners was gone, the three G-men made their way around the mezzanine toward the other side of the jail, where the warden's office was located. Below, in the lobby, they could see the crowd of men receiving their weapons.

Steve turned the knob silently, then eased the door gently open, a fraction of an inch, enough to peer in.

Two people were in there, a man and a girl. The man was tall, muscular, with a high, clever forehead and thin lips. He was holding the girl, whose arm he had twisted behind her in a painful grip. He was holding her with one hand, pushing her imprisoned arm up almost to her shoulder blades, where a little additional pressure would snap it. With his other hand he was holding the telephone.

"It's up to you, Gregg," he was saying into the mouthpiece, "in what shape you want your daughter back. You heard her talk to you. You know we've got the jail covered. You and those cops could never get in here. And while you were trying, your daughter would be screaming—like I made her scream a little while ago, only worse. You can't win, Gregg. You—"

STEPHEN KLAW'S hand tightened on the knob. "Okay, mopes," he said over his shoulder.

He pushed the door violently, and stepped inside.

Bledd jumped up from the desk, dropping the phone and reaching for a gun which lay in front of him. At the same time his hand pushed Susan Gregg's arm further up against her shoulder blade.

Susan gasped, and fainted.

Stephen Klaw stood in the doorway and waited for Bledd to pick up the gun. Then, when Bledd had the weapon pointed at him, Steve raised the muzzle of his automatic, and fired once.

The slug caught Bledd in the stomach, doubling him over onto the desk.

Kerrigan and Murdoch, coming in behind Klaw, looked at Bledd.

"Nice wound," said Murdoch. "He'll live to fry in the chair."

Kerrigan said, "That was lousy shooting, Shrimp. You could have got him in the shoulder just as well."

"Yes," said Steve, "come to think of it, I could have."

Kerrigan picked up the unconscious body of Susan Gregg.

Steve went to the phone and picked it up. He heard Norton Gregg's anxiety-torn voice pounding into the receiver: "Bledd! For God's sake, answer me! What are you doing to Susan?"

"He's doing nothing to Susan," Steve said with a grin. "Come and get her!"

Already there was a rush of feet on the stairs outside, as some of Rory Fenn's men came storming up the stairs.

Out on the mezzanine, Dan Murdoch was coolly picking them off.

Johnny Kerrigan, with the girl over one shoulder, was keeping her body in behind the door of the office while he shot with his free hand.

Stephen Klaw looked around the office, and smiled when he saw what he wanted—a rack of grenades.

He went over and took one. Then he stepped around Bledd's writhing body and went to the door beside Kerrigan.

"Okay," he said. "Let's go!"

Johnny stepped out onto the mezzanine with Steve, and the two of them came up alongside Dan Murdoch, who had just emptied his revolvers. Steve and Johnny kept shooting while Murdoch reloaded. The thugs were coming up the stairs.

Shoulder to shoulder, they advanced to the mezzanine rail,

where they could look down on the massed mob of gunmen below. Rory Fenn was raging.

Kerrigan yelled down, "Hey, Fenn!"

Fenn stopped storming at his men, and they all looked up, weapons raised to shoot. But they let their mouths drop open when Stephen Klaw showed them what he was holding.

"If I pull the pin and drop this down there," he taunted, "you boys know how many of you will be alive one minute after it explodes."

"To hell with him!" shouted Fenn. "He'll never throw it. The explosion would kill them, too. It would wreck the building. He's only bluffing. Shoot! Shoot to kill!"

HE RAISED his own gun, and Johnny Kerrigan, who had been waiting expectantly for that moment, snapped a shot down at him. The steel-jacketed .45 caliber slug tore off most of Fenn's head.

On the heels of the thunderous explosion, Steve Klaw leaned over the railing, with his hand on the grenade pin.

"Throw down your weapons!" he ordered. "Your mayor is our prisoner, and Fenn is dead. You have nothing to gain but death if you resist. Surrender, and you may escape with jail terms if you are not implicated in murder!"

Some half dozen of the men down there began to shout defiance. They were the ones who had committed murder in Bledd's service, and would face death anyway. They wanted to fight it out.

But the other men swiftly overpowered them. In a moment, weapons were dropping to the floor. "We surrender!"

No one moved while Stephen Klaw went down among them, with the grenade still in his hand. They opened a wide lane for him. He went out into the yard and unlocked the main gate to the first of the old-time cops, who were just approaching, led by Norton Gregg.

Gregg tenderly took his daughter from Kerrigan. There were tears in his eyes.

"We're going to re-name City Hall Square after you," he told them. "We're calling it Suicide Square."

"Thanks," said Steve. "You can handle things now. We'll be going. See you soon."

"Where—where are you going?"

Klaw winked at Kerrigan and Murdoch. Then he grinned at Gregg.

"We're going to have a little private celebration with a red-headed girl—in a private rail road car!"

POPULAR HERO PULPS AVAILABLE NOW:

THE SPIDER

- ❏ #1: The Spider Strikes — $13.95
- ❏ #2: The Wheel of Death — $13.95
- ❏ #3: Wings of the Black Death — $13.95
- ❏ #4: City of Flaming Shadows — $13.95
- ❏ #5: Empire of Doom! — $13.95
- ❏ #6: Citadel of Hell — $13.95
- ❏ #7: The Serpent of Destruction — $13.95
- ❏ #8: The Mad Horde — $13.95
- ❏ #9: Satan's Death Blast — $13.95
- ❏ #10: The Corpse Cargo — $13.95
- ❏ #11: Prince of the Red Looters — $13.95
- ❏ #12: Reign of the Silver Terror — $13.95
- ❏ #13: Builders of the Dark Empire — $13.95
- ❏ #14: Death's Crimson Juggernaut — $13.95
- ❏ #15: The Red Death Rain — $13.95
- ❏ #16: The City Destroyer — $13.95
- ❏ #17: The Pain Emperor — $13.95
- ❏ #18: The Flame Master — $13.95
- ❏ #19: Slaves of the Crime Master — $13.95
- ❏ #20: Reign of the Death Fiddler — $13.95
- ❏ #21: Hordes of the Red Butcher — $13.95
- ❏ #22: Dragon Lord of the Underworld — $13.95
- ❏ #23: Master of the Death-Madness — $13.95
- ❏ #24: King of the Red Killers — $13.95
- ❏ #25: Overlord of the Damned — $13.95
- ❏ #26: Death Reign of the Vampire King — $13.95
- ❏ #27: Emperor of the Yellow Death — $13.95
- ❏ #28: The Mayor of Hell — $13.95
- ❏ #29: Slaves of the Murder Syndicate — $13.95
- ❏ #30: Green Globes of Death — $13.95
- ❏ #31: The Cholera King — $13.95
- ❏ #32: Slaves of the Dragon — $13.95
- ❏ #33: Legions of Madness — $12.95
- ❏ #34: Laboratory of the Damned — $12.95
- ❏ #35: Satan's Sightless Legion — $12.95
- ❏ #36: The Coming of the Terror — $12.95
- ❏ #37: The Devil's Death-Dwarfs — $12.95
- ❏ #38: City of Dreadful Night — $12.95
- ❏ #39: Reign of the Snake Men — $12.95
- ❏ #40: Dictator of the Damned — $12.95
- ❏ #41: The Mill-Town Massacres — $12.95
- ❏ #42: Satan's Workshop — $12.95
- ❏ #43: Scourge of the Yellow Fangs — $12.95
- ❏ #44: The Devil's Pawnbroker — $12.95
- ❏ #45: Voyage of the Coffin Ship — $12.95
- ❏ #46: The Man Who Ruled in Hell — $13.95
- ❏ #47: Slaves of the Black Monarch — $13.95
- ❏ #48: Machineguns Over the White House — $13.95
- ❏ #49: The City That Dared Not Eat — $13.95
- ❏ #50: Master of the Flaming Horde — $13.95
- ❏ #51: Satan's Switchboard — $13.95
- ❏ #52: Legions of the Accursed Light — $13.95
- ❏ #53: The City of Lost Men — $13.95
- ❏ #54: The Grey Horde Creeps — $13.95
- ❏ #55: City of Whispering Death — $13.95
- ❏ #56: When Thousands Slept in Hell — $13.95
- ❏ #57: Satan's Shakles — $14.95
- ❏ #58: The Emperor From Hell — $14.95
- ❏ #59: The Devil's Candlesticks — $14.95
- ❏ **NEW:** #60: The City That Paid to Die — $14.95

THE WESTERN RAIDER

- ❏ #1: Guns of the Damned — $13.95
- ❏ #2: The Hawk Rides Back from Death — $13.95
- ❏ #3: Gun-Call for the Lost Legion — $13.95
- ❏ #4: The Law of Silver Trent — $13.95
- ❏ #5: The Gun-Prayer of Silver Trent — $13.95
- ❏ #6: Silver Trent Rides Alone — $13.95

G-8 AND HIS BATTLE ACES

- ❏ #1: The Bat Staffel — $13.95

CAPTAIN SATAN

- ❏ #1: The Mask of the Damned — $13.95
- ❏ #2: Parole for the Dead — $13.95
- ❏ #3: The Dead Man Express — $13.95
- ❏ #4: A Ghost Rides the Dawn — $13.95
- ❏ #5: The Ambassador From Hell — $13.95

DR. YEN SIN

- ❏ #1: Mystery of the Dragon's Shadow — $12.95
- ❏ #2: Mystery of the Golden Skull — $12.95
- ❏ #3: Mystery of the Singing Mummies — $12.95